'Y...   on

thi...   ...'

right?'

'Of course,' Sapphire said, and the vein in her temple pulsed.

It had been her 'give' when she'd been younger—a tell-tale sign that she was rattled—and Patrick didn't know whether to be flattered or annoyed that spending time with him disconcerted her.

'And that doesn't bother you?'

She stood, cool and confident and lithe. 'This is business. Why should it?'

That vein beat to a rap rhythm. *Yeah, she was rattled. Big-time.*

'Okay then, let's do it.'

'Fantastic. You won't regret this.' Her lush mouth eased into a wide grin. 'We're going to be great together.'

'Absolutely.'

And he kissed her to prove it.

Nicola Marsh has always had a passion for writing and reading. As a youngster she devoured books when she should have been sleeping, and later kept a diary whose contents could be an epic in itself!

These days, when she's not enjoying life with her husband and sons in her home city of Melbourne, she's at her computer, creating the romances she loves in her dream job.

Visit Nicola's website at www.nicolamarsh.com for the latest news of her books.

HER DEAL
WITH THE DEVIL

BY
NICOLA MARSH

MILLS&BOON

First published in Great Britain 2013
by Mills & Boon, an imprint of Harlequin (UK) Limited.
Harlequin (UK) Limited, Eton House, 18-24 Paradise Road,
Richmond, Surrey TW9 1SR

© Nicola Marsh 2013

ISBN: 978 0 263 90011 8

Harlequin (UK) policy is to use papers that are natural, renewable and recyclable products and made from wood grown in sustainable forests. The logging and manufacturing process conform to the legal environmental regulations of the country of origin.

Printed and bound in Spain
by Blackprint CPI, Barcelona

Dear Reader

What does romance mean to you?

For me, it's a glance, a smile, a touch, a kiss.

Kisses are special. They convey so much—tenderness and passion, fun and flirting. They're sensual and sexy, sweet and sublime!

Patrick and Sapphire certainly discover all that and more when they join forces for Melbourne Fashion Week. Can the fashion house CEO and the jeweller collaborate in and out of the bedroom?

I love revisiting characters, and was so pleased when Sapphie (who first appeared in MARRYING THE ENEMY, her sister Ruby's story) demanded her very own romantic tale, complete with plenty of kisses…

Happy reading!

Nicola

www.nicolamarsh.com

For my nan, who I miss more than words can say.
Your support for my writing meant so much.
You'll live in my heart for ever.

CHAPTER ONE

SAPPHIRE INTERLOCKED HER fingers and stretched overhead, savouring the slight twinge between her shoulder blades. The twinge was good. It meant her muscles were functioning, which was more than she'd been able to say a few months ago.

But she wouldn't go there. Not today.

Today was all about relaxation and easing back into work. Minimal stress. Positive thoughts. Focus.

She tilted her face to the Melbourne summer sun, enjoying the rays' warm caress.

She should have done this more often. Then maybe she wouldn't have ended up at the brink of collapse and almost losing her cherished family business.

If it hadn't been for her younger sister Ruby... Her shoulder muscles spasmed and she lowered her arms, shook them out, using the relaxation techniques she'd learned during her enforced three month R&R at Tenang, the retreat that had nursed her weary body back to health.

She couldn't afford to get uptight. Not with so much at stake. Not when she had so much to prove in facing her nemesis tomorrow.

With hands on hips she twisted from the waist, deliberately loosening her spine. Some of the tension eased and she closed her eyes, breathed deep. In. Out.

Calm thoughts. Zen. Centred. Relaxed.

'Never thought I'd see the day when the great Sapphire Seaborn connected with her inner yoga chick.'

That voice. No way.

Her eyes snapped open and her Zen evaporated just like that.

Patrick Fourde. Here. In the tiny backyard behind the Seaborn showroom. Seeing her in daggy pink yoga pants, purple crop top and hair snagged in the morning mail's elastic band; not in the fabulous designer outfit she'd planned to wow him with tomorrow.

Freaking hell.

She could feel the blood rush to her face. A virtual red flag to her mortification. Considering their past, she'd be damned if she let him know how truly flustered she was.

The guy had made her last year of high school a living hell and she'd rather grind coal to diamonds with her teeth than work with him now. But she had no choice. She had to reaffirm her leadership of the company. Had to prove she could handle the job physically. Had to ensure she never came that close to losing it again.

She strolled towards him, stopping about a foot away. Close enough to see tiny flecks of cobalt in a sea of grey. His eyes reminded her of a mood stone: bright and electric when he was revved, cool and murky when he had his game face on. Like now.

Lucky for him she'd wised up since high school and could outplay him. Never again would the cocky rebel get the jump on her.

'Was there a problem with our meeting time?'

He grinned—the same wicked quirk of his lips that had driven her batty during Year 12 Biology—and leaned against the doorjamb.

'No problem. I happened to be in the area. Thought I'd drop by for old times' sake.'

This wasn't how she'd envisaged their first meeting after ten years. Not at all.

She didn't like being on the back foot. Not around him. Not when she needed to convince him Fourde Fashion couldn't live without Seaborns' fabulous gems for the upcoming Melbourne Fashion Week.

'Or maybe I couldn't wait 'til tomorrow to see you?'

There it was: the legendary charm. What had it taken? All of five seconds for him to revert to type?

Pity her opinion of the silver-spooned, recalcitrant playboy hadn't changed over the years.

Indulged. Spoiled. Never worked a day in his life. Everything she'd despised in the rich guys she'd grown up with at the private school she'd attended. The type of guys who thought they could snap their fingers and have a harem falling at their feet.

Not her. She'd save her seven veils for strangling him if he didn't agree to her business proposition.

'Still trying to get by on lame flirting?'

'Still the uptight, stuck up prude?'

Ouch. That hurt. Especially as she wasn't the same person—not any more. Working her butt off to learn the family business, losing her mum and having a bruising brush with chronic fatigue syndrome had seen to that.

Besides, she'd never been stuck up or a prude. Uptight? Maybe. But he'd always brought out the worst in her. Riling her with his practised charm, swanning through high school with an entourage of popular kids, teasing her whenever he got a chance.

For some unfathomable reason he'd taken great delight in annoying the hell out of her during their study sessions, succeeding to the point where she'd been flustered and irritable.

The more she'd ignored him, or feigned indifference, the more he'd pushed, niggling until she snapped. Sadly, her cutting remarks would only spur him on, so she'd learned to curb her annoyance and focus on their assignments in the hope he'd get the message.

He hadn't.

She'd become an expert in patience, honing a cool tolerance in an effort to fight back her way.

Until the day she'd had no comeback.

The day he'd kissed her.

'Why are you really here, Patrick?'

'Honestly?'

She rolled her eyes. Did he even know the meaning of the word, with his glib lines and smooth charisma?

'I heard the rumours and wanted to see for myself.'

Uh-oh, this was worse than she'd thought.

She could handle him seeing her without make-up and in workout clothes. She couldn't handle him knowing about Seaborns' reputed financial woes. It would undermine everything and scuttle her entire plan before she'd had a chance to present it.

'You of all people should know better than to listen to a bunch of rumours.'

She attempted to brush past him but he snagged her arm. The zap of *something* was beyond annoying.

Ten years and he still had that effect on her? *Grow up.*

'The reports of my life in the media are highly exaggerated. How about you?'

She could try and outbluff him but, considering she had to meet him at his office tomorrow for the pitch of her life, it wouldn't be the smartest move.

'What have you heard?'

'That Seaborns has been doing it tough.'

'No tougher than most during an economic decline.'

A blatant lie. Not that she'd let him know. If her sister hadn't married mining magnate Jax Maroney the jewellery business that had been in their family for generations would have gone under.

And it would have been entirely Sapphie's fault. She'd been too busy playing superwoman, trying to juggle everything on her own, to let anyone close enough to help. Her stubborn independence had almost cost her the company and her health.

The bone-deep fatigue and aching muscles had scared her, but not as much as the thought that she'd almost failed in making good on her promise to her mum.

No way would she take the business so close to the edge again. She'd do whatever it took—including play nice with this guy.

'Really? Because the grapevine was abuzz with news of Ruby shacking up with Maroney to save Seaborns.'

Bunch of old busybodies—socialites who had nothing better to do than spend their lives sipping lattes, having mani/pedi combos at the latest exclusive day spa and maligning people.

She'd spent a lifetime cultivating friendships in the moneyed circles she'd grown up in, had made an effort out of respect for her mum with Seaborns' bottom line firmly in sight. Rich folk liked to be pandered to, and with the 'old school' mentality at work they stuck to their own. Which equated to them spending a small fortune on Seaborns jewellery.

But it was at times like this, when gossip spread faster than news of a designer sale, that she hated their group mentality.

'You heard wrong.'

She hated having to justify anything to him, but she knew how hard Ruby had fought for Seaborns and she'd do anything for her amazing sister and their company.

The fact that Patrick was partially right—Ruby *had* initially married Jax for convenience to save Seaborns—rankled. If they hadn't fallen head over heels Sapphie would have personally throttled her self-sacrificing sister for going to such lengths for their business.

'Ruby and Jax are madly in love. They can't keep their hands off each other.'

'Lucky them.'

His gaze dipped to her lips and she could have sworn they tingled in remembrance of how commanding his kiss had been for an eighteen-year-old…how he'd made her weak-kneed and dizzy with one touch of his tongue…how he'd made her lose control.

Her lips compressed at the memory. Damn hormones. Just because it had been over a year since she'd been with a guy it didn't mean she had to go all crazy remembering stuff from the past.

Or noticing the way his dark brown hair curled around his collar, too long for conventionality. Or the way stubble highlighted his strong jaw. Or how he never wore his top button done up, making the tanned V of skin a temptation to be touched.

Yep, damned hormones.

'You're flustered.' He took a step closer and it took all her willpower not to step back. 'Anything I can do to help?'

Oh, yeah. But she wasn't going there, and especially not with him.

Once she sealed this deal she needed a date. A hot guy with nothing on his mind but drizzled chocolate and a sleepless night.

As if she'd ever find a guy to live up to her fantasies. The guys she dated were staid, executive types on tight timelines who demanded little. Guys like her.

'Yeah, there is something you can do.' She met his gaze, determinedly ignoring the quiver in her belly that signalled Patrick Fourde would be the kind of guy to make all a girl's fantasies come true. 'Be prepared to be wowed by the best designs Seaborns has ever produced.'

He inclined his head, the sunlight picking up spun gold streaks. 'I'll keep an open mind.'

'That's all I'm asking for.'

'Pity.'

How one word could hold so much promise, so much sizzle, she'd never know. The guy had *suave* down to an art. He'd had that elusive something as a teen and it had evolved into a raw, potent sex appeal that disconcerted her.

Not that she couldn't handle him…it…whatever.

'Did that practised schmooze work for you in Europe?'

Those cobalt flecks flared and an answering lick of heat made her squirm. He didn't speak, and his silence unnerved her as much as the banked heat in his steady stare.

'Because personally it doesn't do much for me.'

'What does?'

'Pardon?'

'What *does* do it for you?' He leaned in deliciously, temptingly close and she held her breath. 'Because I'd *really* like to know.'

His breath fanned her ear, setting up a ripple effect as every nerve ending from her head to her toes zinged.

She could feel the heat radiating off him, could smell a delectable combination of crisp designer wool and French aftershave with a spicy undertone.

Heady. Tempting. Overwhelming.

Powerless to resist, she tilted her head a fraction, the tip of her nose within grazing distance of his neck.

And she breathed. Infusing her senses with him. Closed her eyes. Imagined for one infinitesimal moment what it would be like to close the gap between them and nuzzle his neck.

She had no idea how long they hovered a hair's breadth apart, the inch between their bodies vibrating with an undeniable energy.

'Hey, Saph, you out the back?'

She jumped, snagged her sneaker on a rock and stumbled. His hands shot out to grab her, anchoring her.

She should have been grateful. Instead, with his burning gaze fixed on her, a host of unasked questions she had no hope of answering flickering in the grey depths, she felt embarrassment burn her cheeks.

Patrick Fourde was the master of seduction. Always had been. It came as naturally to him as waking up in the morning. So why the heck was she responding to him on a level that defied explanation?

She couldn't be attracted to him.

Her business depended on it.

Besides, she didn't like him. She'd never liked him. He'd been a major pain in the ass during high school and by the way he'd breezed in here, determined to rile her, it looked as if nothing had changed.

For there was nothing surer—his turning up here today, twenty-four hours before their scheduled meeting, was nothing better than a ploy to unnerve her.

She might need his business, but working alongside him wouldn't be easy.

'Thanks,' she muttered, brushing off his hold in time to see Ruby propped in the doorway, a delighted grin matching the astute glint in her eyes.

'I didn't know you had company.' Ruby winked at Patrick. 'And such fine company at that.'

Debatable.

'Looking good, Rubes.' Patrick saluted her sister. 'Marriage suits you.'

'Thanks.' Ruby's assessing gaze swept over Patrick, and by her growing grin she approved of what she saw. 'Could say the same about you and Europe.'

'Paris is okay, but Melbourne can hold its own.' For some inexplicable reason he glanced her way. 'This city is filled with beauty.'

To her annoyance, Sapphie's blush intensified as Ruby stifled a guffaw.

'You're full of it,' Sapphie muttered under her breath. In

response, he snatched her hand and lifted it to his lips before she could react.

'Maybe so, but you missed me anyway.'

He kissed the back of her hand—a soft, butterfly brush of his lips that almost made her sigh. Almost.

'In your dreams.'

'Count on it,' he whispered, squeezing her hand before releasing it. 'See you tomorrow.'

Damn the man for doing it to her again. Deliberately taunting, trying to make her flustered—and succeeding. Her stupid hand still tingled where he'd kissed it. That whole in-her-face practised French charm…? Yet another of his tricks to tease her. What she couldn't understand was why. Was he trying to get her off-guard before their meeting tomorrow? Trying to disarm her and make her stuff up?

Whatever the answer, she mulled over it while watching one very fine ass as he farewelled Ruby and disappeared into Seaborns on his way out.

Ideally, she would have returned to her relaxation stretches to banish the disturbing sensations Patrick had elicited.

How many times had she done her best to ignore him in Biology, when her recalcitrant lab partner doodled rather than rote-learn the nerves in the human body, would deliberately distract her with stupid jokes, poke fun at everything from her ruled margins to her neat handwriting.

It made what had happened on graduation night all the more annoying, because it had been *him* she'd let her guard down around, *him* who'd been there to offer comfort, *him* who'd made her tingle all over just like the stupid buzz still zapping the skin on the back of her hand.

To add to her discomfort she now had to face a rampantly curious Ruby, who waited until he'd left before bounding towards her.

'Jeez. How seriously hot is Patrick now?'

Sapphie refrained from answering on the grounds that she might incriminate herself.

'I mean he was always hot, with that whole bad boy thing he had going on at school, but now?' Ruby fanned her face. 'He's a babe and he's totally into you.'

Sapphie shook her head and stuffed her hand into her pocket. 'You know better than that. The guy flirts all the time. It's his thing.'

Ruby shifted her weight from side to side, bouncing on the balls of her feet. 'Well, his thing is making you glow.'

'Bull.'

Ruby grabbed her arm and dragged her to a window. 'Go ahead. Look.'

Blowing out an exasperated breath, Sapphie glanced at the glass. Even through a film of dust and rain spots she could see pink cheeks and wide eyes. But it was the expression in those eyes, the glazed confusion of a thoroughly bamboozled woman, that sent her hopes of forgetting the past spiralling on a downward trajectory.

She might despise Patrick and all he stood for, but he appealed to her on some visceral level she had no hope of explaining.

It hadn't made sense back then and it sure as hell didn't make sense a decade later that the guy she could quite happily have strangled had *something* that made her want to explore beneath his flaky surface.

'Been a while since I've seen you look like this. A long while.' Ruby slung an arm across her shoulders and led her inside. 'Suits you.'

'I was doing a few yoga poses outside. That glow...? Must've caught too much sun.'

Ruby laughed and hugged her. 'You're cute when you're in denial.'

'Nothing to deny. Patrick and I will soon be colleagues, hopefully.'

If she hadn't botched it. First impressions counted in her business and considering he was CEO of Fourde Fashion's new Aussie branch, she'd hazard a guess they counted with him too.

Having him discover her in the tree pose, followed by the verbal sparring they'd always been unable to resist, didn't bode well.

At least she hadn't called him any nasty names—something she vaguely recalled doing just before their final exams, when he'd particularly annoyed her with his goofing off.

'Just colleagues, huh?' Ruby bustled into the tiny make-shift kitchen at the back of the showroom and flicked on the kettle. 'Wonder if he'll greet you with a kiss on the hand every day you work together?'

Sapphie's heart splatted at the thought. 'It's a French thing. Means nothing.'

'Hmm…' Ruby popped peppermint teabags into two mugs and propped herself against the bench as she waited for the kettle to boil. 'Wonder if that "thing" extends to French kissing?'

The nibble of a double-coated Tim Tam stuck in Sapphie's throat and she choked, coughing and spluttering, while Ruby poured boiling water into the mugs and grinned.

After a few thumps on her chest, which cleared her throat but did little for her pounding heart and the thought of getting anywhere near Patrick's lips again, Sapphie gratefully took the proffered tea.

'Considering I need to wow him with the presentation to-morrow, you're not helping.'

Ruby's smile waned. 'You're not getting too wound up about this, are you? Because Seaborns is doing okay since the auction and there's plenty of time for you to get back into the swing of things.'

Sapphie cradled her mug, savouring the warmth infusing her palms, and inhaled the fresh minty steam. A sixespressos-a-day gal, she'd never thought it possible she could become hooked on herbal alternatives. But her time out at Tenang had taught her many things—the importance of self-worth being one of the biggies.

She needed to do this, needed to secure Seaborns' future once and for all. Not from any warped sense of obligation to protect her little sister from the hardships of the family business. Not because of the promise she made to her mum on her deathbed.

For *her*. For Sapphire Seaborn, who loved this jewellery company and all it stood for, who secretly wanted her kids to run proudly along these polished floorboards one day, who wanted to prove to herself she didn't have to be a stress-head to be the best in this business and could physically handle the pressures of the only job she'd ever known—the job she valued above all else.

Her brush with chronic fatigue syndrome had left her weak and debilitated. She never wanted to feel that frail again. Ever.

Resuming her position as leader of Seaborns and doing a damn good job was more about proving to herself that she was past her vulnerabilities than anything else.

She had to test her physical capabilities, had to prove she could handle whatever the future held.

'You and Jax pulled off a coup with the auction. Proceeds are still coming in.'

Ruby shrugged, her bashful smirk not fooling Sapphie for a second. Her creative genius sister loved accolades, and the fact that every one of her signature Seaborn pieces had been snapped up at a recent gala auction had ensured orders flooded in. And kept Seaborns viable.

Something she now intended to do. Her way.

'We did okay.' A coy smile curved Ruby's lips. 'For two people who couldn't see what was right in front of their noses 'til it was almost too late.'

Even now Sapphie could hardly believe Ruby and Jax had

fallen in love and made their marriage real in every way that counted. The two were worlds apart yet they connected on a deep emotional level she sometimes envied.

What would it be like to be so into another person you were willing to tie yourself to them to life?

The way she was practically married to Seaborns, she'd probably never know.

'I'm so happy for you.' Sapphie's eyes misted over and she blamed it on the steam from her peppermint tea.

'Thanks, sis.' Ruby sipped at her tea before lowering it to pin her with a probing stare. 'So what are you going to do?'

'About?'

'Patrick Fourde.'

Damn, even hearing the guy's name made her belly knot with trepidation.

'I'm going to make him an offer he can't refuse.'

'Not about work.' Ruby rolled her eyes. 'About what I saw out the back.'

Sapphie didn't want to think about what had happened out the back. She didn't want to give credence to a single thing the flirtatious charmer had said or done.

She surreptitiously rubbed the back of her hand where the imprint from his lips lingered to prove it.

He'd been goading her like in the bad old days, nothing more. The fact she'd let him get to her—not good.

She was older and wiser now. Time to prove she could work with him without letting his deliberate barbs affect her.

'He could be good for you.' Ruby wound the end of her ponytail around her fingertip in the same absentminded way she did while pondering her next creation. 'Bit of fun. Nothing serious. Clear out the cobwebs, metaphorically speaking.'

Sapphie grabbed the nearest teatowel and chucked it at Ruby's head. Her sister ducked, laughing.

'You're right about me needing to date again but I wouldn't touch Patrick Fourde if he was the last guy on earth.'

Ruby smirked. 'Six-month supply of Tim Tams says you can't last a fortnight without getting up close and personal with the dishy Patrick.'

'Too easy.' Sapphie held out her hand to shake on the bet, looking forward to Ruby stocking her pantry with the irresistible rectangles of decadent chocolate. 'You're on.'

Patrick headed for the nearest café. He needed a caffeine shot. Fast. Maybe the jolt to his system would snap him out of his weird funk. A funk that had started around the time he'd laid eyes on Sapphire Seaborn again.

He shouldn't have come, he knew that, but he'd been unable to stay away.

The cool blonde had always had that effect on him. There'd been something about her in high school that had made him want to ruffle her poised, pristine exterior.

Rather than hating the way she'd turned up her pert nose, as if she had better things to do than hang out with him to study, he'd made it his personal mission to see how far he could push before she'd crack.

She never had, and seeing her name on his meeting manifesto was the reason he'd shown up today.

Curiosity. Was she still the same uptight prig? Would he be able to work with her? Seaborns were the best in Melbourne, and that was what he needed for his venture. But being stuck alongside Miss Prissy for the duration of the Fashion Week campaign wasn't his idea of fun.

Until he'd fired his first barb. She'd parried it and had unexpectedly catapulted him back in time. For some unknown, masochistic reason he'd wanted to annoy her all over again for the fun of it.

That kiss on the hand had done it too. He'd seen the initial flash of antagonism in her icy blue stare, the tiny frown between her perfectly plucked brows.

But he'd also glimpsed an uncharacteristic softening, a

thawing of ice to fire, when he'd lingered over her hand, and that had shocked him. Almost as much as his physical reaction.

Hand-kissing a turn on? Who would've thought?

It reminded him of the other time they'd kissed, when he'd managed to delve beneath her frosty veneer and prove she wasn't as immune as she'd like to think.

That was what he had to do if he were to work with her. Keep her off-guard. Maintain control. And show he wouldn't tolerate her coolly disdainful treatment.

This time he had something she wanted and she must want it real bad. For Sapphire to approach *him* for business… Well, Seaborns must be in a worse place than the rumours he'd heard.

Seaborns. He glanced at the elegant art deco cream façade, at the gleaming honey floorboards beneath discreet downlights, at the shimmer and sparkle of exquisite gems behind glass.

And he remembered. Remembered the night he'd brought her home from the graduation dance because her lousy date had been too drunk to drive. Remembered standing in this very spot outside the showroom, reverting to his usual taunts to cheer her up, hating the way the first time he'd seen her vulnerable, seen beneath her outer shell, had made him feel sad rather than victorious.

He remembered the sounds of soft laughter from nearby restaurants, the distinct clang of a tram bell, the faintest wistful sigh a moment before he'd ignored his misgivings and kissed her.

It had been a crazy spur-of-the-moment thing to stop her lower lip wobbling. He'd liked teasing the Ice Princess. He would have hated seeing her cry.

So he'd had no option but to distract her.

He'd expected a kiss to do that and then some.

The part where she'd combusted and he'd lost control a
little... Not supposed to happen.

Who would have thought beneath Sapphire's glacial surface lay a bubbling hotbed of hormones?

He'd kissed a lot of women in his time, in the endless whirl
of parties and fashion events throughout Europe, and dated
some of the hottest women in the world, but that kiss with
Sapphire Seaborn...

Something else.

Not that he deliberately remembered it, but every now and
then, when a blue eyed-blonde gave him a haughty glare, he'd
remember her and that brief moment when he'd glimpsed a
tantalising sliver of more.

Back then she'd shoved him away and fled. Wanting to
ease her mortification—and maybe rub her nose in it a little, because old habits died hard—he'd tried calling once,
e-mailed and texted a couple of times.

Predictably, she'd raised her frosty walls and he'd backed
off. It hadn't bothered him. He'd left for Paris a week later.

Now he was back, ready to take the Melbourne fashion
scene by its bejewelled lapels and give it a damn good shake-
up on his way to achieving his ultimate goal. And if he ended
up working with Sapphire he'd rattle her too.

As he took a seat at an outdoor table at the café next door
and ordered a double-shot espresso he remembered her hor-
rified expression when she'd first caught sight of him.

Shell-shocked didn't come close to describing it.

Only fair, considering he'd felt the same. When he'd first
seen her, arms stretched overhead, revealing a flat, tanned
stomach that extended to her bikini line courtesy of ragged,
low-riding yoga pants, he'd felt like he had that crazy time
he'd leapt into the Seine on a dare: breathless, shivery, out
of his depth.

He'd never seen her so casual or without make-up and it

suited her—as did the layered pixie cut that framed her heart shaped face and made her blue eyes impossibly large.

Usually lithe and elegant, she'd appeared more vulnerable, more human than he'd even seen her, and it added to her appeal.

She'd been hugely confident as a kid. Cutting through a crowd or cutting him down to size. When Sapphire spoke people listened, and he'd been secretly impressed by her unswerving goal to help run the family business.

Not many teens knew what they wanted to do, let alone actually did it, but Sapphire had been driven and determined. And she hadn't had time for a guy who plied his charm like a trade, getting what he wanted with a smile or his quick wit.

So he'd tried harder to rile her, needling and cajoling and charming, buoyed by her reluctant smiles and verbal flayings.

Sapphire Seaborn gave good putdowns.

If it hadn't been for Biology during their final year of high school he would have thought she really didn't like him. But being her lab partner, being forced to work with her, had shown him a different side to Sapphire—one that had almost made him like her.

Because beneath the tough exterior was a diligent, devoted girl who hated to let anyone down. Including him. Probably the only reason she'd put up with him during their assignments.

He admired her unswerving loyalty to her family, her dream to expand Seaborns. Especially when he'd had no aspirations to join Fourde Fashion and all it entailed.

Ironic how, ten years later, he was back in his home city, making Melbourne sit up and take notice of the newly opened Fourde Fashion his priority.

He had a lot to prove to a lot of people—mainly himself—and he'd take Fourde Fashion to the top if he had to wear shot silk and stilettos to do it.

The waitress deposited his espresso on the table and he

thanked her—a second before he caught sight of Sapphire leaving Seaborns.

His gut tightened as she glanced his way, her gaze soft and unfocused, almost lost.

Her vulnerability hit him again. He'd never seen her anything less than über-confident and he wondered what—or who—had put the haunted look in her eyes.

She hadn't caught sight of him so he stood and waved her over.

A slight frown creased her brows as she worried her bottom lip, obviously contemplating how to flee. He took the decision out of her hands by ordering a tall, skinny, extra hot cappuccino with a side of pistachio *macaron*, loud enough for her to hear.

Her eyes narrowed as she stalked towards him, the yoga pants clinging to her lean legs like a second skin, a pink hoodie hiding the delectable top half he'd already checked out.

Sapphire might be petite, but the way she held herself, the way she strode, made her appear taller. In heels, she was formidable.

He liked the grass-stained purple sneakers with diamante studs better.

'Care to join me?' He pulled out a wrought iron chair. 'I ordered your favourites.'

'So I heard.' She frowned, indecisive, as she darted a glance inside. Probably contemplating how to cancel the order without offending. 'Rather presumptuous.'

He pointed to his espresso. 'I hate drinking alone.'

'I'm busy—'

'Please?'

He tried his best mega-smile—the one she'd never failed to roll her eyes at.

She didn't disappoint, adding an exasperated huff as she slid onto the seat. 'Tell me you're not still using that smile to twist people around your little finger.'

He shrugged. 'Fine. I won't tell you.'

'Does it still work?'

'You tell me.' He crooked a finger, beckoning her closer. 'You're here, aren't you?'

'That's because I haven't had my cappa fix this morning.'

'And you can't resist anything sweet and French.'

She snorted. 'Surely you're not referring to yourself?'

'I've lived in Paris for ten years.' He leaned towards her, close enough to smell the faint cinnamon peach fragrance of her shampoo—the same one that had clung to his tux jacket after their kiss. 'And you used to find me irresistibly sweet.'

She pretended to gag and he laughed.

'Let me guess. You're trying to impress me by remembering my favourites after all these years?'

'Not really.' He pushed around the sugar sachets in the stainless steel container with his fingertip. 'Hard for a guy to forget when you had the same boring order every time we studied for those stupid Biology spot tests.'

She ignored his 'boring' barb. Pity.

'Remember the plant collection assignment?' She winced. 'Just thinking about poison ivy makes me itchy.'

'Though it wasn't all bad.' He edged closer and lowered his voice. 'As I recall, the human body component in last semester proved highly entertaining.'

Her withering glare radiated disapproval. The arrival of her coffee and *macaron* saved her from responding.

He let her off the hook. Plenty of time to stroll down memory lane if she wowed him with her presentation, as he expected, and they ended up working together.

It would be interesting, seeing if the old bait and switch that had underpinned their relationship in high school would apply now. If her responses to him so far were any indication, not much had changed. He relished the challenge of making her loosen up. She thrived on proving that anything he said annoyed the crap out of her.

She'd change her attitude if Fourde Fashion brought Seaborns on board for this campaign. And if that happened he should change his attitude too.

He needed this business venture to thrive, and he needed to be on top of his game to do it. Invincible. And he knew Sapphire could help him do it.

There might not have been so much at stake in high school, bar a pass or fail grade, but he hadn't forgotten her ability to command and conquer. If she brought half that chutzpah to her presentation tomorrow he had a feeling Fourde Fashion working with Seaborns for Fashion Week couldn't fail.

And that, in turn, would launch his plans—the ones ensuring the entire fashion world, including his folks, would finally forgive the mistakes of his past and recognise there was more to him than his family name.

'Fill me in on what you've been up to.'

An eyebrow inverted as she stared at him over the rim of her cappuccino glass. 'In the last decade?'

'Give me the abbreviated version.'

'The usual. Taking over the business. Working my butt off to make it thrive.' Shadows darkened her blue eyes to midnight before she glanced away.

Damn. How dumb could he be? He'd forgotten all about passing on his condolences. 'Sorry about your mum.'

'I am too.' She cradled her coffee glass, determinedly staring into its contents.

'You must miss her?'

'Every day.'

With a suddenness that surprised him she placed her glass on the table and jabbed a finger in his direction. 'Her drive and vivacity and tenaciousness were legendary. And that's exactly what you'll get a taste of in my presentation tomorrow.'

'I don't doubt it.'

He was surprised by her mood swings: pensive one mo-

ment, wary the next. The old Sapphire would never let anyone get under her guard—least of all him.

Which begged the question: what had happened to make
her so...*edgy*?

'No significant others?'

A faint pink stained her cheeks again, highlighting the
incredible blueness of her eyes—the same shade as the precious stone she was named after.

'Haven't had time.' She picked up her glass again, using
it as a security measure. 'Work keeps me busy.'

'Will you fling that *macaron* at me if I quote you the old
"all work and no play" angle?'

'No, because I've heard it all before.' Her fingers clutched
the glass so tightly her knuckles stood out. 'Besides, I play.'

Defensive and nervous. Yep, definitely not the woman he
remembered.

'How?'

She frowned. 'How what?'

'How do you play? What do you do for kicks?'

The fact that she screwed up her nose to think and took
for ever to answer spoke volumes.

'You're a workaholic.'

She puffed up with indignation. 'I do other stuff.'

'Like?'

'Yoga. Pilates. Meditation.'

He laughed, unable to mesh a vision of the long-striding,
book-wielding girl going places with an image of Sapphire
sitting still long enough to contemplate anything beyond Seaborns' profit margins.

'What's so funny?'

He shrugged and stirred his espresso. 'You're different
than how I remember.'

Tension pinched the corners of her mouth. 'I was a kid
back then.'

'No, you were a young woman on the verge of greatness.

And I'm having a hard time reconciling my memory of you then with who you are now.'

He willed her to look at him, and when she did the fear in her gaze made him want to bundle her into his arms.

Closely followed by a mental *what the hell?* He'd learned the last time that Sapphire didn't value his comfort and he'd be an idiot to be taken in by her vulnerability again. For all he knew she could be using it as a ploy to soften him up before the presentation tomorrow.

'I'm still the same person in here,' she murmured, pressing her hand to her chest. But the slight wobble of her bottom lip told him otherwise.

She wasn't the same, not by a long shot, and it irked that deep down, in a metrosexual place he rarely acknowledged, he actually cared. Crazy when he didn't really know her, had never known her beyond being someone to tease unmercifully for the simple fact she'd made it easy.

He could have probed and prodded and grilled her some more, but she seemed so defenceless, so *broken*, he didn't have the heart to do it.

So he reverted to type.

'Maybe it's the casual exercise gear that threw me?' He winked. 'I much prefer you in a school uniform.'

'You're a sick man,' she said, the glint of amusement in her eyes vindication that he'd done the right thing in not pushing her.

'Well, then, maybe you should don a nurse's uniform instead and—'

'Unbelievable.' She pursed lips in disapproval and his chest tightened inexplicably. 'You haven't changed a bit.'

'You have.' On impulse he touched the back of her hand and she eased it away, grabbing a teaspoon to scoop milk froth off the top of her cappuccino.

'Ten years is a long time—what did you expect? To find me dissecting frogs and acing element quizzes?'

He couldn't figure why she vacillated all over the place but there was something wrong here, some part of the bigger picture he wasn't seeing, and if he were relying on her to help push Fourde Fashion into the stratosphere he needed to know what he was dealing with.

It was good business sense. It was an excuse for his concern and he was sticking to it.

'Did you stop to consider my kiss may have ruined you for other men?'

Her eyes widened in shock at his deliberately outrageous taunt a second before she picked up several sugar sachets and flung them. He caught the lot in one hand.

He'd wanted a reaction and he'd got it. It was a start.

'Newsflash: that kiss meant nothing. You caught me at a bad time and it ended up being two hormonal teens making out in a moment of madness.' She crossed her arms and glared, outraged and defiant. 'And I think it's poor form, you bringing it up a decade later when we're potentially on the verge of working together.'

'Another thing that's changed. You used to be brutally honest. Saying that kiss meant nothing?' He tsk-tsked. 'Never thought I'd see the day when you told a fib.'

He baited her again, wondering how far she'd go before he got a glimpse at the truth. He moved the sugar out of her reach just in case.

'I'm not playing this game with you.' She slammed her palms on the table and leaned forward, blue eyes flashing fire. 'No reminiscing or teasing. No pretending to be buddies. And definitely no talk of kissing.'

She waved a hand between them.

'You and me? Potential work colleagues. Our aim? To make our businesses a lot of money. So quit pretending to be my best buddy, because I don't need a friend—I need a guarantee.'

Ouch. This brutal honesty he remembered.

'Of what?'

'That you'll give me a fair hearing tomorrow and you'll judge my presentation on merit and not on our past rel— friendship.'

'You can say it, you know.' He cupped his hands around his mouth to amplify his exaggerated whisper. '*Rel-a-tion-ship.*'

When she swore, he almost fist-pumped the air. This was more like it. Sapphire riled and feisty. He could handle her this way, firing quips and barbs to get a rise. The withdrawn, almost melancholic woman she'd been a few minutes ago confused the hell out of him.

'This is important to me,' she said, her tone low and ominous. 'You may have it easy, being given a subsidiary of your folks' company to play with while you're in Melbourne for however long you care to stick around. Me? Seaborns is everything, and I'll do whatever it takes, including aligning our jewellery with your fashion, to ensure my company is never threatened again.'

Not much made Patrick quick to anger—bar anyone casting aspersions on how hard he worked.

He'd had a gutful of people doubting him. Doubting his capabilities, doubting his creativity, doubting his business brain.

It was why he'd leapt at the chance to head up this new branch. It was why his main goal was to show the world what he was made of. He intended to prove all the doubters wrong—including his parents.

Patrick Fourde had left the mistakes of his past behind and he had what it took to be a success beyond the family name and all it stood for.

'Are you done?'

Something in his tone must have alerted her to his inner frustration, for she slumped back into her chair and held up her hands in surrender.

'Sorry.'

'No, you're not. You believe all that crap.'

Just as his folks believed Jacques had single-handedly come up with the concept for the spring collection that had set the couture gowns sales in Paris soaring.

It had been the first time in ten years they'd given him another chance to work on a primary showing, collaborating on the spring collection alongside Jacques. Maybe they expected him to be eternally grateful, maybe they expected him to stuff up again, but never had they considered for one second *he'd* been the creative genius behind it.

He'd waited for their acknowledgment that he'd made amends for his monumental stuff-up when he'd first started with the company, waited for an encouraging word.

All he'd got was begrudging thanks for being part of a successful team.

Pride had kept him from confessing his true role and he'd realised something. Until he proved he'd put the past behind him *on his own* no one would believe him.

Least of all himself.

And it was at that moment he'd made his decision.

Making a success of the Australian branch of Fourde Fashion wasn't debatable. It was imperative.

He needed to do this.

For him.

He'd accept nothing less than being the highest-grossing branch in the company—and that included topping their long-established French connection. Closely followed by putting his secret plan into action.

And he was looking at the one woman who could help make that happen.

'You think I'm some lazy, indulged, rich playboy who gets by on his charm and little else.'

She couldn't look him in the eye—vindication that he was spot-on in her assessment of him.

'You never did give me any credit.'

Her mouth opened and closed, as if she'd wanted to respond and thought better of it. But her eyes didn't lie, and their shameful regret made him want to thump something at the injustice of being judged so harshly.

'Irrelevant, because my work will speak for itself.'

He expected to see scepticism.

He saw admiration and it went some way to soothing his inner wildness.

'Okay, then, I guess we both have something to prove.' She nodded, tapped her bottom lip, pondered. 'From here on in a clean slate.'

'No preconceptions?'

'None whatsoever.'

For the first time since he'd sought her out today a coy smile curved her mouth, making him wish she'd do it more often.

'Though you *do* rely heavily on charm.'

'Pity it never worked on you,' he muttered under his breath, surprised by her sharp intake of breath, as if she'd heard him.

She downed the rest of her cappuccino in record time and scooped the pistachio *macaron* into her palm. 'Gotta dash. I'll see you tomorrow afternoon.' She cocked her finger and thumb at him. 'Prepare to be wowed.'

As he watched her stroll away, the Lycra clinging to lean legs and shapely butt, he wondered what she'd think if she knew she'd already achieved her first goal.

CHAPTER TWO

'YOU'D THINK AFTER three months at a freaking health spa I'd be more relaxed than this.'

Sapphie glared at Karma, the goldfish she'd purchased after checking out of Tenang as part of her new calm approach to life.

Right now rainforest sounds spilling from her iPod dock, lavender fumes from her oil burner and talking to Karma weren't working.

She'd never felt so tense in all her life and she had Patrick Fourde to blame.

The guy was infuriating.

The guy was annoying.

The guy was seriously hot.

And that was what had her flustered deep down on a visceral level she didn't want to acknowledge.

Despite his inherent ability to consistently rub her up the wrong way, even after a decade, she found him attractive.

That ruffled, casual, bad-boy aura he had going on? Big turn-on. *Huge.*

It was why she'd deliberately held him at arm's length during high school.

Patrick Fourde, in all his slick, laid-back glory, had encapsulated everything she'd yearned to be and couldn't. She'd had major responsibilities, being groomed to take over Seaborns, and while she'd relished every challenge her mum had thrown her way she'd always secretly wanted what Patrick had.

Freedom.

Freedom to be whomever she wanted, whenever she wanted. Freedom away from maternal expectation. Freedom from being Sapphire—the eldest, responsible one. The confident, competent one. The driven, dependable one.

She'd envied Ruby for the same reason, loving her carefree, creative sister but wishing she could be like her.

It was why she hadn't burdened Ruby with the promise she'd made to their mum on her deathbed, why she'd kept Seaborns' economic situation a secret until it had been too late.

She'd learned the hard way how foolish it was to do it alone, to hide her stress beneath a brittle veneer, and if she hadn't almost collapsed with fatigue she might have jeopardised the company altogether.

The fact she'd ignored the signs of her ailing body, pushing herself to the limit with the help of caffeine drinks and energy bars, foolish behaviour she'd never accept with anyone, least of all herself. But she'd done it—driven her body into the ground because of her stubborn independence.

Thankfully she'd wised up, vowed to take better care of her body.

She never, ever wanted to experience the soul-sapping fatigue that had plagued her for weeks when she'd first checked into Tenang. The nebulous chronic fatigue syndrome—something she'd heard bandied around on current affairs programmes but knew little about—had become a scary reality and she'd fought it for all she was worth.

When she'd left Tenang she'd promised to take time out, to achieve a better balance between her business and social lives.

Karma gaped at her, opening and closing his fishy lips, and she could imagine him saying, *So how's that working out for you?*

She'd been back on the job a week, easing into the business by scouring accounts, re-establishing contact with clients and making projections for the next financial year. It had been going well, coming to work in casual workout clothes and sneakers, wearing no make-up, not having to put on her 'company face' for clients and the cameras.

Being CEO and spokesperson for Seaborns had always given her a thrill, but the stress of possible financial disaster had ruined her enjoyment of the job.

While Seaborns had recovered, courtesy of Ruby and Jax, she'd never let the situation get out of hand again. Which was why she'd latched onto the idea of working alongside Fourde Fashion for the upcoming Melbourne Fashion Week.

A mega seven days in the fashion world, it would secure Seaborns' future for ever if their exquisite jewellery designs were seen with designer clothes from Fourde's.

Despite their past, she hadn't hesitated in contacting Patrick's PA for an appointment when she'd heard the CEO of Melbourne's newest fashion house was courting jewellers for a runway partnership.

Patrick's terse, impersonal response had surprised her but she hadn't cared. She had her chance.

So why had he shown up at Seaborns yesterday, seemingly hell-bent on rattling her?

If his wicked smile and smouldering eyes hadn't undermined her, his ability to hone in on how much she'd changed would have.

How had he done that?

The guy she'd known had never pushed for answers, had never bothered to be insightful or concerned. He'd teased and annoyed and badgered his way through their year as lab partners in Biology, never probing beneath the surface.

She'd pretended to tolerate him back then, when in fact— she could finally admit it—she'd looked forward to their prac sessions with a perverse sense of excitement. Biology had been the relief of her senior year. Through the heavy slog of

Maths and Economics and Politics—subjects recommended by her mum and careers adviser, she'd craved the tantalising fun she'd have with Patrick.

It had been a game with him back then. A challenge for him to rile her into responding. She hadn't given him the satisfaction most of the time, choosing to ignore him as a way of dealing with his constant outrageous annoyances. But she'd seen his respect on the odd occasion she'd snapped back, and for some bizarre reason she'd valued it.

He'd made her rigid life bearable. Not that she'd ever let him know. The more he teased and taunted the harder she'd pushed him away.

Until graduation night. The night she'd let down her guard and he'd swooped, making a mockery of her stance to ignore him.

She'd never had a boyfriend in high school, had never been kissed before that night. And the fact Patrick had been her first had really peed her off at the time.

She'd blamed him. *He'd taken advantage of the situation. He'd seen her at her worst and had kissed her as part of his usual taunts. He'd probably laughed at her afterwards.*

But none of that had been true. In reality he'd been gallant in bringing her home after her date ended up drunk. And his kiss had been one of comfort, not cruelty.

It wasn't his fault she'd gone a little nuts.

That was why she'd ignored his overtures to meet after that night. Pure mortification. And a small part of her knew she would have hated having him belittle something as special as that spectacular first kiss.

He would have too, to lighten the mood between them— would probably have been as embarrassed as her and covered it by taunting her.

Thankfully he'd given up after a week, headed to Paris, and she'd forgotten about it.

Until now.

Beyond annoying.

She glanced at the alarm clock next to the bed and winced. Less than an hour until her pitch.

Yesterday had been an aberration. The feeling that she'd connected with him on some deeper level that went way beyond their banter in high school hadn't happened. It had been a figment of her imagination—the same imagination that insisted she go out and find the hottest guy in Melbourne to have some fun with.

That was what their tenuous bond had been about: her need for some male company and his inherent ability to flirt with anything that moved.

Harsh? Yeah. But it was the only way she'd cope with the riot of uncertainty making her doubt her choice of outfit, accessories, and the wisdom of meeting up with him—albeit for work.

'This is business.' She squared her shoulders. 'I can do this.'

Karma's affirmation consisted of a gill twitch as he ducked behind his treasure chest.

At least she looked the part. Knee-length, A-line sleeveless dress with a fitted bodice and cinched waist in the deepest mulberry, towering stilettos in black patent, and an exquisite amethyst pendant on a simple white gold necklace with matching earrings.

Throw in the dramatic make-up, designed to accentuate her eyes and lips, a hairspray-reinforced slicked-back coif that could withstand the stiffest breeze, and she was ready to face him.

This was how she'd envisaged their first meeting after a decade: with her power-dressed, strutting into his office, demonstrating her control and confidence and *savoir-faire*.

Considering he'd seen her in her oldest yoga pants and a crop top yesterday she'd kinda lost her advantage.

Then she remembered the look in his eyes when he'd first

seen her, as if he'd wanted to gobble her up and come back for main and dessert… Maybe she still held the upper hand after all.

Not that she'd stoop so low as to use her sexuality to seal a business deal, but knowing the great and powerful Patrick found her attractive made her walk that little bit taller.

'Wish me luck,' she said, snatching up her bag and smoothing her hair one last time.

Karma gave a lazy swish of his tail. No problem. When she stalked into Patrick's office shortly armed with a presentation to wow him, she'd have all the good karma she needed.

She'd make this Fashion Week deal happen.

Let him try to stop her.

'The pieces are good. Really good.'

The fact that Sapphire sat close to Patrick on his office sofa, her stockinged leg within tantalising touching distance, was not so good.

How was a guy supposed to concentrate?

The moment Sapphire had strolled into his office, looking as if she'd stepped off the pages of a fashion mag, he'd been befuddled.

There was nothing revealing in her outfit but the cut of the fabric and the way she wore it made him think of the screen sirens of old. Beautiful, curvaceous women who were proud of their bodies and weren't afraid to flaunt them in understated elegance.

And stockings… He loved them—the sheerer the better. None of those thick opaques for him. The way they added a sheen to Sapphire's legs, highlighting their shape…and the possibility that she might be wearing suspenders to hold them up…

Another thing he'd discovered since she'd arrived: hardons were distracting and guaranteed to scuttle a business meeting.

His plans to take the Melbourne fashion scene by storm would be derailed before he'd begun if he started thinking with the wrong head.

'These pieces are some of Ruby's best work, but she's willing to design whatever you want—depending on the concept you come up with.'

Her eyes sparkled with enthusiasm and he wondered if they darkened when she was aroused.

Hell. Still thinking with the wrong head.

'The show's next month. Sure you can deliver?'

He hated how abrupt he sounded, but he needed to refocus and stifle the urge to readjust his pants.

'Definitely. We'll work nights, do whatever it takes.'

'You want to be on the runway alongside Fourde that badly?'

A flicker of fear shimmered in her defiant gaze before she blinked, leaving him wondering if he'd imagined it.

'Yeah, I want Seaborns to be featured with your designs. I'm a savvy businesswoman and, as you know from the suitors bashing down your door, any jeweller in this city would give their last diamond tennis bracelet to accessorise your clothes.'

He admired her honesty. But she was right. He'd had back-to-back meetings all day in which he'd been systematically wooed and impressed by the calibre of jewellers in Melbourne.

The city might not have the same *joie-de-vivre* as Paris but it had certainly come a long way since he'd lived here.

The fashion scene thrived, with worldwide designers setting up shop, which was the only reason his folks had deemed it prudent to launch a branch of Fourde Fashion here.

With Jerome, his older brother, heading Milan, and his younger sister Phoebe heading New York, he'd been the only one left to thrust into a makeshift CEO position.

Not that he was complaining. He'd been desperate to prove

he could do this. The disaster of his first campaign had seen to that.

He knew they thought he was only a figurehead, a puppet whose strings they could yank at will. They'd even installed Serge, the manager of Fourde's flagship store near the Champs-Élysées, alongside him.

Apparently Serge '*had the expertise*' and was '*worth his weight in gold*' despite the fact he and Serge, his best mate, had cut a path through Paris, Monte Carlo, Nice, Barcelona and most of the other cities in Europe together, living the high life, partying their way through each country.

He'd done it in an attempt to shrug off the taint of his first showing, wanting to be known for something other than his notorious failure.

It had worked too. His socialising antics had been diligently reported and the press had soon forgotten the savaging he'd received at their hands following a mistake that had cost Fourde Fashion megabucks.

He'd eventually returned to the company in different roles, learning what he could without being given any real responsibility.

It had suited him. Given him time to re-evaluate personally what had gone wrong. But no matter how many times he tried to analyse it, no matter how many angles he considered, it all came back to one thing: he'd tried to take an established brand and create something new that wouldn't fit.

His parents had given him free rein for his first showing, wanting to see what he came up with, and he'd been determined to show them what he could do.

Correction: he'd wanted to wow them. He hadn't had their attention in years—they'd moved to France for their precious business when he was still a teenager, had barely acknowledged their late-life 'mistake' for years before that—and he'd wanted to make a major impression.

He'd done that all right. For all the wrong reasons.

He'd swapped the Forde designs for ones he'd planned as part of a small group of designers. A catastrophic move that had cost the company a small fortune and pretty much sealed his career where his parents were concerned.

He'd been a fool to think Fourde Fashion was ready for cutting edge contemporary, and the fact his folks had distanced themselves from him—*'to protect the company,'* apparently—still burned after all this time.

It shouldn't have come as any great surprise. They'd been emotionally distant for as long as he could remember. Not from any deliberate cruelty but for the simple fact that their business came first. Always.

Birthdays and Christmases were spent having snatched lunches and the obligatory presents before they headed back to the office. Phoebe and Jerome were used to fending for themselves and his parents had expected him to do the same despite their fourteen-year age-gap.

He'd been the baby they'd never expected to have in their mid-forties. He got it. He'd grown used to their absence early on.

But when he'd finally joined the fold and wanted them to sit up and take notice of his talents, of *him*, it had been a flop.

Their continued lack of appreciation of his efforts, their distrust of his talents, all stemmed from his first failure, and despite how hard he'd worked since they couldn't forget it.

Well, the success of Melbourne Fashion Week would make them forget.

He'd make sure of it.

'What can you offer me that the other jewellers can't?'

Her eyes widened imperceptibly before her gaze dipped momentarily to his lips, and for one crazy, irrational second he wished she'd make an offer that had nothing to do with business.

'One hundred percent commitment.' She tilted her chin

up and eyeballed him. 'I'm willing to do whatever it takes to have our designs accessorising yours.'

'Anything?'

Until now he'd been the epitome of a corporate businessman, with his mind on the job. But with a hard-on that wouldn't quit, her body enticingly close, and her tempting cinnamon-peach fragrance wrapping him in an erotic fog, he couldn't help but flirt.

Besides, that was what she thought he was—an idle playboy who'd never worked for anything in his life. He'd gladly disillusion her. Later.

Now, he wanted to play a little.

'Within reason.' A tiny frown slashed her brows and she held up hand between them.

Yeah, like *that* would stop him.

'Hmm...' He drummed his fingers against his thigh, pretending to ponder. 'I could get you to privately model a few designs.'

Her frown deepened and her lips thinned.

'Or you could help me with the lingerie line.'

She didn't speak, but the daggers she shot him with her narrow-eyed glare spoke volumes.

'Or we could get together in my penthouse suite and do some serious—'

'Stop toying with me.' She jabbed at his chest. 'You want the best? Seaborns is it and you know it.'

She snatched her hand away when he glanced at it, still lingering on his chest.

'Quit stalling. Do we have a deal or not?'

With her eyes flashing indigo fire, her chest heaving from deep breaths and her designer-shoe-clad foot tapping impatiently an inch from his, she was utterly magnificent.

Once again she brought to mind starlets of old: glamorous, powerful women who knew what they wanted and weren't afraid to go after it.

That was when it hit him.

The idea that had been playing around the edges of his mind, taunting him to grab it and run with it.

'You're a frigging genius!' He grabbed her arms so suddenly she was startled, and his maniacal laughter sounded crazy even to his ears.

'You're out of your mind.' She brushed him off with a slick move that suggested martial arts training. 'Just tell me already.'

He leapt from the sofa and started pacing, riotous ideas peppering his imagination. He needed to sit, jot them down, make some sense of the brainstorm happening in his head.

This was what had happened in Paris, when he'd nailed the spring showing.

He'd done it. *His* ideas. *His* campaign. Not that upstart smarmy Jacques with his stupid berets and fast talking.

This creative freefall had also occurred for his first showing too—*the one that must not be named*, as he'd labelled it in his head following the shemozzle.

The spring collection might have gone some way to restoring his confidence, but it was this show that would prove beyond a doubt that he had what it took to make it in the fashion world.

With Sapphire Seaborn along for the ride every step of the way.

He stopped in front of her, itching to get started. 'You know we'd be working on this project twenty-four-seven, right?'

'Of course,' she said, and the vein in her temple pulsed.

It had been her 'give' when she'd been younger—a telltale sign that she was rattled—and he didn't know whether to be flattered or annoyed that spending time with him disconcerted her.

'And that doesn't bother you?'

She stood, cool and confident and lithe. 'This is business. Why should it?'

That vein beat to a rap rhythm. Yeah, she was rattled. Big time.

'Okay,' then, let's do it.'

'Fantastic. You won't regret this.' Her lush mouth eased into a wide grin. 'We're going to be great together.'

'Absolutely.'

And he kissed her to prove it.

CHAPTER THREE

SAPPHIE'S FIRST INSTINCT was to knee Patrick in the groin. But he'd probably enjoy the contact too much.

She settled for placing both palms on his chest and shoving—hard.

'Can't blame a guy for wanting to celebrate the most significant moment of his career.'

The fact he was still using that boyish grin to try and disarm her a decade later made her want to knee him again.

As for the flutter low in her belly? It was a reminder that she hadn't eaten lunch and nothing to do with the insistent tug of attraction between them.

An attraction torched to life by his kiss.

Why did the most annoying guy on the planet also have to be the best kisser?

It didn't make any sense. She'd barely given him a second thought all these years—discounting the first few months after he'd left—yet all it took was one smooch—okay, one pretty scorching smooch—to resurrect how amazing he'd made her feel with his first kiss.

She could kill him.

Willing her pulse to stop pounding, she glared at him through narrowed eyes. 'You do that once more and I'll take Seaborns jewellery and walk.'

He merely raised an eyebrow, not in the least intimidated by her bluff. 'You need me as much as I need you, sweetheart.' She gaped at his insolence and he laughed. 'Come on, you know better than to con a con. I'm blunt. I say it as it is. You and me?' He waved a hand between them. 'We're going to take Fashion Week by storm, so don't let your predictable outrage over a little spur-of-the-moment celebratory kiss get in the way of a beautiful friendship.'

Predictable outrage? She shook her head, unsure whether to applaud his honesty or reconsider that knee to the balls.

She had to regain control of this situation—fast—and the way to do that was to focus on business.

Not the naughty twinkle in his grey eyes.

Not the smug smirk quirking his lips.

Not the way he continued to stare at her mouth as if he was primed for a repeat performance.

'What's with the *"most significant moment of your career"* big talk?'

For the first time since she'd entered his ultra-modern office he appeared a tad uncertain, tugging at the cuffs of his shirt.

'I've been looking for an angle for Fashion Week—something to play to the company's strengths.'

'And?'

His gaze raked over her but there was nothing overtly sexual about it. Maybe she'd imagined his hungry stare a moment ago. In fact he seemed to be sizing up her outfit and accessories in a purely professional manner.

'When you first walked in here you made a statement.' He tilted his head to one side, evaluating. 'Class. Elegance. Timeless. Made me think of screen legends in the past.'

A compliment from a guy who threw them out there like confetti. Who would have thought it?

'Should I be flattered or concerned you just called me old?'

The corners of his mouth quirked. 'You don't need to fish for compliments. You're stunning and you know it.'

Actually, she didn't. The designer clothes, the jewellery,

the make-up and hair were all part of her duties as spokesperson for Seaborns. Take away the fancy outer dressing and she was Sapphire Seaborn—the responsible one, the devoted one, the sensible one. She didn't do outrageous things. She dated *suitable* men and socialised with a *suitable* crowd.

Spending more than five minutes in the company of Patrick Fourde was decidedly *un*suitable. Or, more to the point, it elicited decidedly unsuitable thoughts.

He'd always had that effect on her. Been able to confuse and bamboozle and intrigue her with the barest hint of that lazy half-smile he had down pat.

She might have been immune in the past, but having him in her face again—bolder, brazen, still bamboozling—unnerved her far more now than he ever had.

'Get to the point.'

He stalked around his desk and fired up his laptop, swivelling the screen to face her.

'Bear with me a sec.'

His fingers flew over the keyboard and, increasingly curious, she propped herself on the edge of his desk.

The tip of his tongue protruded slightly as he concentrated on typing and her chest tightened in remembrance.

He'd used to do the same thing when they studied together. She'd known when he'd stopped goofing off—which had been rarely, admittedly—and started taking their studying seriously by that tell, and it was as endearing now as back then.

At the time, she'd done her best to give him the impression she couldn't stand the sight of him. Had berated him constantly about slacking off and sketching instead of studying. Her chastisement had only served to stir him up further and he'd deliberately make fun of her work or call time out for a coffee.

Interesting how his doodling had probably been a prelude to his career in fashion, an outlet for his creativity. And to see him now, CEO of a branch of a world-renowned fashion house, made her feel ashamed she'd given him such a hard time.

Then again, considering the amount of time he'd spent poking fun at her study timetables and subject spreadsheets, her guilt quickly faded.

Whatever he was doing now, it had captured his attention and given her an opportunity to study him. In his flawlessly fitted charcoal suit and open-necked black shirt, perched behind a glass-topped desk large enough to fit an entire classroom, with the skyline of Melbourne surrounding him with three hundred and sixty degrees of floor to ceiling windows fifty storeys high, he looked like the consummate businessman.

A guy on top of the world, in total control and loving it. Who would have guessed the laid-back charmer had ambition?

He'd never shared any of his plans with her—had never showed any interest in business beyond teasing her about taking such a manic interest in Seaborns.

She'd been surprised when he'd absconded to Paris—had assumed it had been to live the high life on his family money.

After that first kiss she'd reluctantly kept an eye on him, had followed him on the internet for six months, surprised by mentions of him doing an internship at Fourde Fashion headquarters.

Pity those internet hits had also shown her the type of life she envied: parties and nightclub openings and theatre galas. The type of life she'd secretly craved but had been too focused on work, on proving herself, on seeking approval, to do anything about.

How different would her life have been if she'd let go just a little? Had hung out with Patrick for fun, not study? Responded to his teasing with smiles, not frowns? Allowed herself to indulge in a few wild teenage stunts without thought for the consequences?

Maybe she wouldn't have ended up stressed, repressed and almost losing the company.

'Here. Take a look.' He pointed at the screen, filled with images of stunning screen sirens.

Grace Kelly. Eva Marie Saint. Ingrid Bergman. Audrey Hepburn. Marilyn.

She knew them all, had shared her mum's love of old films, but had no clue why he was showing her these pictures.

He must have read the unasked question in her eyes for he grabbed a pen and notepad and started scribbling.

'Tell me the first words that pop into your head when you look at those women.'

It would be a lot more fun brainstorming if she knew what he was getting at but she'd play along for now.

'Stylish. Chic. Classy.'

'Exactly.'

He continued jotting, muttering under his breath. The tip of his tongue was back and she couldn't help but smile. If he was this enthused now, she had full confidence their joint collaboration would steal the show.

'This is my significant moment.' He twirled the pad so she wasn't reading upside down. 'Hollywood glamour of old.'

She squinted at his illegible notes as he flung the pen down and stood.

'We go all out. Elegant clothes. Curvy models. Bold colours and designs. Dramatic make-up.'

He started pacing and she'd never seen him so focussed.

'A theme to make people wish they'd lived decades ago. We play on the fashion frenzy *Mad Men* has recreated but take it a step further back in time. When women were proud to be sensual and lush and weren't afraid to hide the fact.'

For some reason heat crept into her cheeks at the way he said *sensual*. Jeez, what would it be like to have a guy like him go all sensual on her?

Yeah, *that* was helping her blush.

'Rich fabrics. Satin. Lace. Hugging curves. Fitted pencil skirts. Long elbow gloves. Hourglass silhouettes.'

He fired the words out at random, his eyes sparking with passion, and the heat in her cheeks spread to the rest of her body.

She literally tingled with the urge to touch him, to see if the powerful vibe emanating from him would zap her.

If he were this passionate about work, how worked up did he get in the bedroom?

She swallowed. It did little to ease the sudden dryness in her mouth. The exact opposite in other areas of her body.

She really needed a date desperately if she were having illicit fantasies about the guy who drove her mad.

'You like the idea.' He grabbed her hand and twirled her, and she couldn't help but laugh. His enthusiasm was infectious.

'What gave it away?'

'This.' He trailed a fingertip from the outer corner of her eye, down her cheek and around her lips, tracing their shape with exquisite precision. 'When you're relaxed your face lights up.'

'Probably a reflection of yours,' she muttered, knowing she should step back and put some much needed distance between them, but captivated by the incredible longing she glimpsed in the depths of his gaze.

He had to be longing for success, not her, right? The guy who'd squired starlets to gallery openings and models to movie premieres. The guy who'd cut a path through Europe with his legendary parties. The guy who'd teased her incessantly at high school.

They couldn't be attracted; it wouldn't be prudent.

But the longer they stood like this, invisible energy crackling between them, his fingertip lingering at the corner of her mouth, which he now stared at as if he wanted to devour it, the more she knew she was kidding herself.

Working with Patrick was going to be a living nightmare.

She stepped back and forced a smile. 'You're right. This idea is fabulous.'

'Great.'

He picked up his notepad, but not before she'd glimpsed confusion creasing his brow. Join the club.

She'd always labelled their relationship as volatile. He'd taunt her, she'd fake aloofness, until they reached an *impasse* fraught with unresolved tension. At least on her behalf. For being around him back then had made her tense in a way she couldn't describe. It had gone beyond exasperation at his deliberate teasing, had left her feeling...*frustrated.*

She'd put it down to being a hormone-ridden teen with a secret passion for romance novels and no time to date. And she was beyond grateful he'd never seemed clued in to her dissatisfaction.

He'd never given any hint he liked her as more than a friend, and she'd been deluded enough to believe her self-talk that she didn't like him *that* way.

But she had.

It was why that kiss on graduation night had meant so much. And why she'd freaked out because of it.

Because a momentous kiss like that had the power to change dreams and hers had already been set in stone.

She would be the next CEO of Seaborns.

Nothing—no one—could change that.

So why the relentless *yearning* now? The feeling that she'd missed out on something and regretted it?

It annoyed her, this uncertainty. Usually she knew what she wanted and made it happen. Yesterday.

She didn't like doubting herself. Or him, for that matter. And she did. A small part of her wondered how the larrikin teen could morph into this determined businessman and pull off something this big.

Having an inkling he was in this position purely because

he'd got the job handed on a silver platter from his folks and having her suspicions confirmed by asking him was mutually exclusive. She couldn't ask without alienating him or emasculating his pride and potentially stuffing this collaboration up before they'd really begun.

But she had to voice some of her doubts, couched in business terms.

'While I think something like this could cause a sensation at Fashion Week, and make the world sit up and take notice of our companies, do you think it's too ambitious?'

He glanced up from his notepad and stared at her as if she'd suggested he don one of the dresses.

'One thing I've learned in this biz is to dream big. Go all out. Make an impact.'

He knew. Knew she doubted him. She saw it in the slightly narrowed eyes, the disappointment pinching the corners of his mouth.

'If you're questioning my credentials, why did you come here in the first place?'

Yep, he was mad. She'd never heard his voice like this: hard, flat monotone with a hint of ice.

'I'm not questioning—'

'Yeah, you are.'

He flung the pen he'd been holding onto his desk and raked a hand through his hair, ruffling the too-long-to-conform whorls.

'Here's a newsflash. Don't believe everything you read in the press, because sometimes it's what goes on behind the scenes that counts.'

Oo-kay, so that was cryptic. What did his social antics have to do with work?

'Besides, you know me—always the risk-taker.' He stabbed a finger at the scrawl-covered notepad. 'Thinking big is what's going to have every person in this city and beyond talking about Fourde Fashion, and that's my number one goal.

To go places.' He eyeballed her with a steely determination she hadn't known he had in him. 'And if you're smart you'll be along for the ride.'

Sapphie didn't know how smart it was being tied so closely to Patrick for the next month but she did know business, and every cell in her body was screaming that this deal was the opportunity of a lifetime.

'The new me is in favour of risks.' She held out her hand to shake on it. 'Let's make this happen.'

As Sapphire chatted with Ruby on the phone, outlining the basics and the timeframes involved to ensure their proposal hit the ground running, Patrick surreptitiously studied her.

What had she meant, '*the new me*'?

Apart from a shorter layered haircut and a few more blonde streaks she looked as if she hadn't aged a day since he'd last seen her.

Though the curves were new. And that look in her eyes...

He couldn't put his finger on it but, while she looked the name on the outside, he had a feeling she'd gone through some major stuff to put that bordering-on-haunted gleam in those big blue eyes.

Not that she'd tell him. She seemed determined to keep him in the same box she'd constructed for him back in high school. The one labelled 'Lazy Lout Happy to Coast on his Family's Fortune'.

He'd pretended it hadn't bothered him back then, had gone out of his way to tease her for being the opposite—'Little Miss Prissy Being Groomed to Follow in Mama's Footsteps'.

But now? Yeah, it bothered him. He'd had a gutful of being labelled and misjudged by everyone from the paparazzi to his folks. Especially his folks.

Ironic that growing up he'd craved their attention, and yet when they'd finally given it, it had been for all the wrong reasons.

To have Sapphire echo their doubts felt as if someone had slugged him in the guts.

For some unfathomable reason her opinion mattered after all this time. It shouldn't. They were now business colleagues.

The irrefutable, irrational urge to rip her clothes off and devour her didn't come into it at all.

Sex without complications. That was what he wanted, and for one insane moment earlier, from the way she'd been looking at him, he'd almost say she wanted it too.

For Sapphire wouldn't have room in her well-ordered life for complications. He respected that about her—her focus on her job. He'd met women like her around the world—high-fliers who took no prisoners, who didn't have time for emotional entanglements, who were happy being independent and forceful and in control.

Not every female needed a wedding ring and kids to feel validated, and by Sapphire's go-get-'em attitude, she'd chosen to marry her career instead.

She glanced at him and rolled her eyes, imitating Ruby's garrulousness with her hand. He mimed hitting the disconnect button and she smiled—a genuine, dazzling display that left him slightly winded.

Sex without complications, remember?

Sleeping with Sapphire wasn't wise. That was one giant complication just waiting to happen.

She *had* changed. The Sapphire he'd known would never have taken time out to do yoga, let alone be seen dead in leisure clothes. When she hadn't been in school uniform she'd worn tailored pants and button-down shirts, appearing way older than her years but making it work regardless.

She hadn't cared what other kids thought of her, and while their rich, indulged classmates at the exclusive school they'd attended had been boozing and partying their way through high school she'd been friendly yet aloof, happy in her own skin, proud of her choices.

He'd envied her that—her certainty in knowing what she was going to do with her life. He hadn't had a clue, and had taken the Fourde internship by default, accepting it when a PR job at a Paris magazine had fallen through.

And look how that had turned out.

Maybe he would have been better staying well away from the family business but despite what had happened he didn't regret the years he'd spent at Fourde.

He wouldn't have discovered his talent for taking conceptual ideas and seeing them through to fruition. He wouldn't have discovered his passion for brainstorming and elaborating and collaborating. And he wouldn't have known he had the creative spark passed down in his genes if he hadn't been surrounded by the passion of Fourde Fashion on a daily basis.

A huge part of him was grateful for the opportunities he'd been given, but another part wished he'd been brave enough to put his plans in motion earlier.

Seeing his folks in action had gone some way to soothing his resentment. If they'd been time-poor with him when he was growing up, they were frenetic now. They never stopped. Working eighteen hour days. Rarely taking time to eat. Grabbing coffee and croissants on their way between meetings.

Their dedication to Fourde explained why they'd missed his first footy game—missed the whole season—why they'd never shown up at his school presentations, why he'd thought eating dinner alone was the norm until one of his school buddies had invited him around to his place one night.

It had sucked at the time, fending for himself, and their neglect had fed his antipathy. But working alongside them in Paris had shown him it wasn't personal. They didn't have time for anyone unless it involved Fourde's.

Were they selfish and self-absorbed? Hell, yeah.

Malicious? No.

And his tense relationship with his folks had more to do

with people co-existing but not really knowing each other
than any residual bitterness on his behalf.

That didn't stop him wanting to prove how damn good he
was, and that was exactly what he'd do with Sapphire's help.

'Done.' She slid her phone back into her handbag. 'Ruby's
hyped. She's on the Net as we speak, researching the general
feel of old Hollywood glamour, and she'll start doing some
virtual mock-ups for you to take a look at by tomorrow.'

'Wow, no grass growing under her feet.'

He watched her walk towards him, gorgeous in designer
mulberry and high heels, and all that self talk about not going
there was gone in the few seconds it took for a hard-on of
mammoth proportions to return.

Gritting his teeth against his apparent lack of self-control,
he turned away to look out of the window.

He had to hand it to his folks. Nothing but the best for
Fourde Fashion, with this sky-high office on the top floor of
one of Melbourne's newest developments. Though he knew
his fancy office had more to do with maintaining the image
behind the Fourde name than any caring for him on their part.

Fourde Fashion needed a presence in Australia. He was it.
They didn't expect soaring profit margins or breakout collections. They'd be happy with same-old, same-old and a steady
cashflow from a market they deemed insignificant at best.

Lucky for them he never settled for anything but the best.
Ever. He would never accept failure again, and he intended on
proving that to everyone—including the woman now standing by his side.

Her subtle cinnamon fragrance teased his senses and he
curled his fingers into his palms to stop himself reaching
for her.

Maybe he should sleep with her and be done with it?

'Some view.'

He grunted in response, surprised when she laid a tentative hand on his arm. Yeah, *that* was helping.

'What's wrong?'

'You really want to know?'

'Wouldn't have asked if I didn't.'

He dragged in a breath, another, staring at the iconic city landmarks so many floors down. Flinders Street Station, Federation Square, St Patrick's Cathedral—buildings he'd explored as a kid on school excursions, usually with this woman by his side.

What the hell was he doing, contemplating telling her the truth? It wouldn't end well.

But he knew one thing for sure. He couldn't go on like this.

It had been two measly days since he'd marched back into her life, and this relentless, driving urge to have her wasn't going away any time soon. In fact it would probably intensify the more time they spent together working.

Probably best to get it out of his system? Then focus one hundred percent on blowing the competitors away?

But how did he tell her without sounding like an ass?

Hey, Saph, the reason I keep kissing you—can't keep my hands off you. Want into your pants. Now.

Yeah, that would go down a treat.

'Not like you to be at a loss for words.' She removed her hand and he instantly wished he'd grabbed it and held on. 'Maybe working with you is going to be tolerable after all?'

A reluctant chuckle spilled from his lips and he turned to face her.

And that was when he knew he couldn't tell her about his driving need to ravish every inch of her body.

Staring into her guileless eyes, seeing concern clouding their perfect blue, he couldn't do it.

Ten years had passed, but how well did he really know her? If she'd freaked out back then, what was to say she wouldn't do it now and jeopardise the entire showing?

He needed this Hollywood glamour idea to fly. He needed to wow audiences and critics and guarantee that orders flooded in. He needed to show everyone he wasn't the wealthy flake they wrongly assumed.

And that meant focussing on the goal and not on his rampant libido.

'We have to make this work. It's important to me.'

Her eyes widened in surprise, as if she'd doubted his sincerity before but didn't now.

'Me too,' she said, her nod brisk and businesslike. 'You meet with your designers, I'll put the PR machine in motion, and we'll reconvene later today.'

'Sounds like a plan.'

He liked plans. Plans were orderly and well thought out and logical. The opposite of the uncertainty rioting through him.

'We should do dinner.'

It was a vast improvement on what he really wanted to say: *We should do each other.*

A tiny crease reappeared between her brows. 'A working dinner, you mean?'

He'd prefer something along the lines of cosy and candlelit, with the two of them naked, but he'd settle for working. It was the one thing to keep him focussed away from wanting her, right?

'We'll be working long into the evening—stands to reason we need to eat.'

'Okay, then.'

She'd reverted to brusque and he mentally kicked himself for wanting what he couldn't have.

'Meet back here at five?'

He glanced around the room, at the contemporary sterility, and made a rash decision he'd probably live to regret.

'How about we meet at Seaborns? That way you can show me what Ruby has in mind for some of the major pieces?'

'Sure, that's doable.'

There he went again. One word—*doable*—and he could see the two of them *doing* each other.

'Better get cracking.'

He mentally cringed at how abrupt he sounded, not surprised when she shot him a sideways glance.

But in true Sapphire form she didn't push the issue or demand answers. She picked up her portfolio, hoisted her handbag onto her shoulder, and headed towards the door.

With her hand on the doorknob, she paused. 'Want to hear something crazy?'

Crazier than how badly he wanted her?

'Yeah?'

'I'm actually looking forward to this.'

Her impish grin as she eased through the door made him want to stride across the office and haul her back in.

She wasn't the only one looking forward to the month ahead.

Who said he couldn't mix a little pleasure with business?

CHAPTER FOUR

RUBY AND OPAL had a plate of double-coated Tim Tams waiting for Sapphie when she got back.

They'd closed the showroom and were lounging around the makeshift living room near Ruby's studio. It was a new addition in her absence and, while she liked Ruby having a place to chill between inspiration hits, it reminded her of her failure.

She should have been here.

Instead she'd been recuperating after being an ass, not trusting Ruby enough to share the responsibilities of running Seaborns, and driving herself into the ground because of it.

If she hadn't wound up chronically tired, her body aching all over, barely able to lift her head off the pillow because of the headaches… No, she wouldn't think about the possible consequences of her controlling behaviour. Not today, when hopefully she'd ensured that Seaborns would never face the threat of closure ever again.

She'd been so stupid, thinking she could control everything. Lucky for her, her body had sent out some pretty powerful warning signals, and she'd listened before the chronic fatigue syndrome had really taken hold.

For weeks before she'd finally admitted defeat she'd existed on caffeine energy drinks and liquid vitamins, trying to push through the tiredness, taking on a bigger workload.

It wasn't as if she'd never been tired before. Running a

business took its toll, and she'd been used to functioning on minimal sleep and snatched meals.

Until her body had other ideas.

She'd pulled yet another all-nighter after a long week of meetings with accountants and suppliers, had been in the process of downing her second energy drink for the morning, when she'd fainted, clipping her head on the corner of her desk on the way down.

Ruby had heard the noise, panicked when she'd found her unconscious and called an ambulance.

She'd come to before the paramedics arrived, but by the hard glint in Ruby's eyes Sapphie had known her number was up and she couldn't fool anyone any longer.

The paramedics might have pronounced her vital signs to be sound, but that hadn't stopped Ruby badgering her into a doctor's visit and a thorough physical.

Sapphie had barely got through the preliminaries before admitting defeat. Her body simply hadn't been holding up under the pressure she was placing on it.

If Ruby's scathing scolding hadn't convinced her to take three months off and check into a health spa the doc would have.

The moment she'd heard the long-term repercussions of CFS she'd booked a place at Tenang ASAP. Ongoing joint pain, visual disturbances, recurring sore throats, chronic cough, chest pain, allergies, depression... She'd asked the doc to stop around then, wishing she hadn't been so stubborn in shouldering Seaborns without real help.

She'd had a lucky escape, had listened to her body's symptoms in time, but every morning when she woke she experienced a moment of fleeting panic that maybe she wasn't as strong as she thought she was.

She went through the same daily routine now: deep breaths, ten in total, pushing her abdomen out, filling her lungs. Followed by pointing her toes towards the end of the bed five times, contracting her leg muscles. Bicycling in the air, loosening up her back. A few gentle reps of abdominal curls, finished with a hands-overhead stretch from top to bottom.

It had become a ritual, a way of ensuring her muscles woke slowly before she actually got out of bed, a way of caring for them when she hadn't before.

The regular meditation and yoga sessions had helped her reconnect with her body too, and she actually looked forward to the muscle-twanging stretches and peaceful interludes within a busy day.

As for her diet, she'd ditched the caffeine, always managed to scrounge three small protein-rich meals a day and drank her weight in filtered water.

She needed her body in tip-top working order, and making Seaborns successful now had more to do with proving that her physical strength hadn't diminished as keeping a promise to her mum before she'd died.

Ruby patted the sofa next to her. 'Take a seat and tell us everything.'

Where should Sapphie start? The part where Patrick had kissed her again and she'd let him? Or the part where they almost needed a force field to keep them from ripping each other's clothes off whenever they got within two feet?

That meeting in his office had been horrendous—much worse than she'd anticipated. Not on any professional level, he'd seriously impressed her there, but for the simple fact she couldn't explain where the heady sexual tension had sprung from.

If she'd had to deal with that during Year 12 she would've failed Biology for sure.

He wasn't helping matters either, playing up to it. Not that she should be surprised. It was what he did.

But her reaction… The flushed skin, the sweaty palms, the buzz thrumming her body… Inexplicable.

She couldn't afford to be attracted to Patrick—not when they'd be working on this campaign together.

Try telling that to her body.

And that was what bugged her the most. She'd been going to great lengths to take care of her body yet in one hour he'd managed to make her feel alive in a way she hadn't for a long time.

She could put it down to endorphins, the euphoria associated with nailing her presentation, but what was the point in lying?

Her body had hummed because it strained to be naked with Patrick's, endorphins or not.

'There's not much to tell,' Sapphie said, hoping her cheeks wouldn't show a betraying blush.

'Yeah, and I'm about to abseil down the Eureka Towers wearing nothing but a tiara,' Ruby said, shaking her head. 'You know we'll make it up if you don't tell us.'

Sapphie settled for the abridged version.

'Patrick came up with the idea of old Hollywood glamour as the lynchpin of his Fashion Week show.' She cradled her tea, the warmth a welcome infusion for her icy hands. They matched her cold feet after spending too many hours one-on-one with the guy who made her body hum just by being near him. 'I think it's fantastic.'

'Sure is.'

Opal slid the plate of Tim Tams across to her and Sapphie took two, demolishing the first before the chocolate oozed onto her fingers.

'This is going to gain recognition for Seaborns overseas. I just know it.'

'Great going.' Ruby nudged her with an elbow. 'Now tell us the rest.'

Opal stifled a giggle and Sapphie glared at her sister. 'What have you been saying?'

'Nothing.'

Ruby's deliberately wide eyes and *faux* innocent smile wouldn't have fooled anyone. 'When our lovely cuz was helping me do inventory I happened to mention the way Patrick looked at you yesterday.' Ruby pointed at Opal. 'Not *my* fault if she jumps to conclusions.'

Opal snorted. 'If memory serves correctly, you were the one waxing lyrical about Saph *"needing to get some"* and Patrick being *"just the guy to give it to her"*.'

Sapphie glared at Ruby. 'Tell me you didn't say that.'

'Okay, then, I won't tell you.' Ruby winked and crammed another Tim Tam into her mouth while Sapphie resisted the urge to bury her face in the nearest cushion to hide any incriminating blushes.

Opal studied her over her skinny latte before placing the coffee glass on the table. 'We looked him up Saph, and I have to say he's incredibly hot. If he's half as good in person as he is on screen...'

Great. Just what she needed. Her cousin and her sister joining forces in trying to get her laid.

'I used to dissect frogs with the guy. It kinda takes the shine away.'

'Bull—' Ruby covered the rest of her declaration with a fake sneeze. 'I saw the way you looked yesterday after he'd dropped around.'

'Tired and frazzled?'

Ruby made a buzzing sound. 'Incorrect. Try perky and glowing.'

'You're full of it,' Sapphie said, glancing at Opal for support.

She shrugged and picked up her coffee to hide a burgeoning grin.

'Okay, then, let's look at this rationally.' Ruby elbowed her. 'You've been recuperating for months, and for half a year before that you were steadily driving yourself into the ground—

which is why you almost ended up with severe chronic fatigue syndrome.'

Sapphie opened her mouth to respond but Ruby held up her hand.

'During that time you didn't date. You didn't eat either. But that's another lecture you've already had.' Ruby tapped her bottom lip, pretending to ponder. 'And, as I recall, one of the things you said when I picked you up from Tenang two weeks ago was, "I really need a date—bad."'

'You said it. *Date* being the operative word. *Date*—not business colleague.'

'That's beside the point and you know it.' Ruby dunked a Tim Tam in her espresso. Pushy and sacrilegious. 'It's not like you guys are strangers. You hung out all through senior year—'

'Once again, that was for *work*. We were Biology lab partners, that's all.'

Ruby waved the Tim Tam around; it would serve her right if it softened, and the dunked bit fell off and landed on the floor.

'I'm not that much younger than you, Saph, and I remember the way you'd be after *studying* with him.'

Sapphie clamped her lips shut. Of course she'd looked different after studying with Patrick. The guy had driven her insane with his lack of concentration and constant distractions.

'You'd look the same way you did yesterday. *Glowing.*'

Sapphie waited until Ruby had stuffed the Tim Tam into her mouth so she couldn't respond.

'I was a serious student and Patrick's mission in life was to make our study sessions as hard as humanly possible. He was a pain in the ass. Who may have made cramming for exams bearable with his bickering. So that glow was probably relief that for a few hours a week I could forget about everything else and just be a kid, maybe even laugh a little.'

Ruby's hand paused halfway to her mouth as Opal darted confused glances between them.

'As for yesterday? Already told you. I probably caught too much sun while doing yoga out the back.'

Opal smirked at that one, while Ruby shook her head. 'You know how I feel about you shouldering the load and the unrealistic expectations Mum put on you. Not fair. Not by a long shot. So the fact Patrick made you laugh…don't you want to recapture that feeling again?'

Ruby didn't have to say it but the rest of her sentence hung in the air, unsaid… *After all you've been through?*

She knew Ruby wouldn't let this go until she gave her a snippet of truth. "Course I want to feel carefree, but that's just it, Rubes. All the meditation and yoga and Pilates in the world aren't going to change facts. Sure, I've learned to chill, but I am who I am, and the best way for me to start feeling good again is to do what I do best. Work. Run Seaborns. Contribute.'

Ensure she could cope physically with the demands of a job she loved.

That was what had scared her most during recovery—hoping her body could keep up with her mind.

She had so many plans she wanted to instigate, so many ways to ensure Seaborns stayed on top in the jewellery business, but she wouldn't be able to do a darn thing if her body let her down.

Hopefully, with a little TLC, her battered body would be back to its invincible best soon.

'Crazy workaholic,' Opal muttered, pretending she didn't see the death glare Sapphie shot her.

'You can still do all those things and have fun,' Ruby said, slinging an arm across her shoulders. 'The thing is, if you're so busy working and getting this showing together, how will you have time to find a date? Bonking Patrick kills two birds with one stone—'

'How about killing two family members with one stone?' Sapphie jabbed a finger at the octagonal lapis lazuli pendant hanging around her sister's neck. 'That's big enough to do the trick.'

Opal laughed and pointed at Ruby. 'She started it.'

Ruby chuckled and squeezed her shoulders. 'Think about it, okay? You're busy but you need to have a little fun. Patrick seems like the perfect solution.'

Unfortunately Sapphie happened to agree.

She could protest all she liked but Ruby made sense. She'd be working on this showing with him twenty-four-seven. She wouldn't have time to socialise let alone date.

Would it be so bad to give in to a little harmless flirtation?

Only one problem. Considering how her body came to life around him, how harmless would the flirtation be?

Several hours later Patrick questioned the wisdom of meeting Sapphire at her place to work.

Keeping his hands off her in the sterility of his office had been difficult enough without this…this…cosiness.

Meeting at the Seaborns showroom should have been entirely business-focussed. Instead they'd reported their day's progress in an hour and made an agenda for tomorrow in the following thirty minutes. Leaving him pacing the tiny apartment over the showroom while she *slipped into something more comfortable.'*

Yeah, she'd actually said those words, completely ingenuous—until he'd snorted. Only then had recognition dawned.

She'd rolled her eyes at him, accused him of having a filthy mind and strolled into the bedroom, slipping off her towering ebony patent leather pumps along the way.

The black seam of her stockings, starting at her heel and running all the way up her legs and underneath her knee-length crimson skirt had not helped the filthy mind situation.

If any other woman had uttered those words he would have

been prepped for a bout of wild sex. Coming from Sapphire, after ninety minutes of work focus, he acknowledged it for what it was. The simple statement of a tired workaholic who wanted to change out of her business suit.

He knew the feeling. Following her example, he unknotted his tie and stuffed it into his jacket, hanging on the back of a chair. He unbuttoned his cuffs and rolled them up to his elbows but stopped short of slipping off his pants. Time enough for her to see his boxers.

Chuckling under his breath at what she'd think of that cocky declaration, he wandered around the apartment. The place wasn't like Sapphire at all, with its ethnic cushions in bright colours, mismatched multi-coloured bottles serving as vases and a stack of chick-flicks in towering disarray next to an ancient DVD player.

She'd told him Ruby used to live here, before she'd moved out recently to be with her husband, and that Sapphire found it convenient while she eased back into the business.

When he'd asked why she had to ease back she'd clammed up and made a big deal of going over their itineraries for the next week.

Discomfort had made her babble so he'd let her off the hook. For now. Day two of the frantic month's work ahead wasn't the best time to be interrogating his colleague. He'd bide his time. Maybe a fine bottle of Grange wouldn't go astray?

Great, not only was he assuming he'd get her naked, he wanted to get her drunk too.

Way to go with his reformation.

Those days of carousing were long behind him. He'd grown tired of the paparazzi's constant scandalmongering in Paris, had found their scrutiny of his social life tiresome. Sure, his lifestyle had served its purpose, getting them to focus on his wild ways rather than that botched first showing, but it had reached a stage where he hadn't been able to travel through

Europe without some journo assuming it involved a woman, a secret assignation, or both.

And when there was nothing they simple invented it. Funny how one mistake in his past had long-term ramifications. Despite him towing the company line for many years now, he'd never shaken the feeling the paparazzi were one step away from reviving the disaster of his early show.

So he'd played up to the party animal image, hung around Serge despite the two of them growing apart in the maturity stakes, because it had been way easier being seen as a playboy than as a disillusioned guy out to prove himself.

His parents had written him off a long time ago, so nothing he'd done socially mattered. As long as he stuck to the rules where Fourde Fashion was concerned they were happy.

Those rules were mighty restricting, and not conducive to creativity, but he'd done what he had to do the last few years to regain respectability in a cut throat industry that didn't give too many second chances.

It had been part of his long-term goal to become a valued member of Fourde Fashion, because no way could he pull off his plans unless he had an established name in the biz.

After the *'flamboyant, avant garde, cutting edge'* show that had cost the company thousands when he'd first started, he'd learned to bide his time.

He'd known the fashion world would be ready for a contemporary transformation eventually. It was just a matter of when. Lucky for him, that time was now.

He'd watched the tide turn in Europe with increasing excitement. Sure, there would always be a place for classic couture houses like Dior, Chanel and Fourde Fashion, but an influx of young designers had seen a few indie collections that made his blood fizz with anticipation.

The modern wave wasn't taking over the catwalks yet, but give it time. And he intended on cresting that wave with contemporary designs the fashion world had never seen.

Opening a branch of Fourde Fashion in Melbourne couldn't have come at a more opportune time. It gave him time to prove he could launch a successful solo show and lend kudos to his upcoming venture.

The one driving force behind everything he did these days.

He picked up a photo of Sapphire and Ruby, with their arms slung across each other's shoulders outside the gigantic laughing mouth of Luna Park, and rubbed the dust off the glass with his thumb. It must have been taken a few years after he'd left. Ruby looked in her late teens, Sapphire early twenties, but the age difference was more pronounced by the worldly expression on Sapphire's face.

She didn't look like a young, carefree woman having a fun day hanging out with her sister at a St Kilda amusement park. The slight crease between her brows, the rigid posture, the half-smile screamed too much responsibility.

He should know. His siblings had worn the same expression since the time they'd graduated from high school and gone straight into the fashion business, taking night courses to stock up on their theoretical knowledge while working alongside their folks during the day. Before they'd all moved to Paris, leaving him behind.

He'd thought it pretty cool at the time, being trusted enough to live with a dotty aunt who didn't care what time he got home from school or who he brought with him. At least that was what he'd told himself in order to handle the seething emotions he'd hidden deep down.

Though what had he expected? Considering his folks' focus on Fourde Fashion, it shouldn't have come as any great surprise that they'd left him behind.

His family were virtual strangers. Living in the same house, barely conversing. Jerome had sat him down when he'd turned twelve and told him the cold, hard facts. With two teenagers, their folks hadn't banked on having a third child—a 'mistake'. They had goals to achieve and glass ceilings to shatter.

Jerome's advice had been simple: if he didn't expect anything he wouldn't be let down.

He'd remembered that when they'd left him behind, but it hadn't made the pain any easier.

They'd cited a logical reason, of course: wanting him to finish his education at the prestigious private school so he had a *'good grounding in order to enter the family business'* when he joined them.

No choice. An order. One that he'd been determined to ignore until he'd got lousy grades for his final exams and realised he'd rather be doing something creative than bumming off his folks.

When he'd joined them in Paris and the PR magazine job had fallen through he'd been determined to prove his worth. He'd been given free rein to demonstrate what he could do and ended up costing the company and losing his parents' respect because of it.

In not following protocol, being cocky and over-confident, he'd let his family down. And it seemed as if nothing since had been able to convince them of his seriousness when it came to work.

The long hours he put in, the extra duties he assumed, the collaborations he worked on—all had garnered the barest of recognition from his folks. Sure, they'd given him an end-of-year-bonus like the rest of their workers but the acknowledgement he secretly craved, where they'd recognise his creativity as being ahead of its time, had never come.

Until he'd realised something. He could never be who he truly wanted to be while under the Fourde Fashion brand.

For that was all his parents cared about: living up to their name, producing the same kinds of clothes with a different twist according to season and year. They wanted to deliver on the promise of sameness, while he longed to be different.

It made good business sense, and their long-standing reputation in the fashion industry was testament to it but he was tired of being part of a crowd.

He wanted to stand out—wanted his designs to stand out.

But first he had to ensure Fourde Fashion in Melbourne produced the best show Fashion Week had ever seen.

His swansong for Fourde's and a launching pad for him.

Doubts plagued him—had he read the fashion scene correctly or was the timing all wrong again—but he'd never know unless he tried.

He'd mentioned leaving the company to his folks and they'd hardly blinked. No begging him to stay. No heaping praise on him as a valued worker. They'd given him the customary brush-off with *'we'll discuss this later'* and assigned him to head up the Melbourne office.

If they thought the token CEO role would make him stay with the company, they were mistaken.

He appreciated the opportunity, but that was all it was. An opportunity for bigger and better things. Done his way.

And then he'd put his other plans into action.

'Don't know about you but I'm starving.' Sapphire padded silently into the room, barefoot, hair down, clad in worn denim and a teal tee, and he took extra care replacing the photo on the table, so he wouldn't give away the slight tremor of his hands. Hands that wanted to be all over her.

She frowned when she noticed he'd been checking out old photos. 'I'm ordering take-out. You're welcome to stay.'

He should go.

He should grab his stuff, head for the office, and bury himself in work all night in an effort to forget how sweet and tousled and *available* she looked right at this very minute.

He should remind himself how important this showing was, and how getting involved with Sapphire Seaborn on any level other than business was a monumentally daft idea.

'Sounds good,' he said, silently cursing his weakness when it came to this intriguing woman.

'Fancy anything in particular?' She rifled through a stack of restaurant flyers next to the phone, glancing up when he didn't answer.

She had Indian in one hand, Thai in the other, and all he could think was how he'd like to devour *her*.

His hungry gaze started at her feet, the high arches and long toes, moved up legs encased in denim that could have been poured on, skirted around the area that had driven his decision to stick around, lingered on her small, firm breasts before eventually meeting her eyes.

He'd expected censure and condemnation for his blatant perving. He hadn't expected an answering heat that had him hard in a second.

If she gave him a sign—any sign—that she wanted this as much as he did he'd vault the sofa and take her up against the wall.

He willed her to say something, to be brave enough to articulate what was zapping between them.

For the decision had to come from her. He knew what he wanted—hot, wild sex—but would she view it the same way?

Sapphire was so intense, so focussed, would she read too much into a quickie to take the edge off?

He'd never mixed business with pleasure before, had turned down numerous models, campaign managers and even rival CEOs. It never did to complicate matters. But this time with Sapphire he'd compartmentalise.

But would she be able to do the same?

His fingers curled into his palms and he clenched his hands into fists, holding himself perfectly still. He couldn't afford movement, for when he did move it would be in a beeline straight for her.

Their gazes locked for an eternity—his taunting her to accept his unspoken dare, hers surprisingly bold.

He waited, unaware he'd been holding his breath until she broke the deadlock and his lungs emptied in a rush.

'I fancy Thai.'

Not quite the *I fancy you* he'd been hoping to hear and not half as satisfying he'd hazard a guess.

As she studied the menu with intense fascination he came to a lightning quick decision—the kind of impulse he'd been famous for in his wilder partying years, the kind of decision that had made Paris sit up and take notice of his first dramatic show. Not in a good way.

But this was different. He was a decade older, a decade wiser. And going after Sapphire because he wanted her was a purely primal drive he needed to slake before it became an obsession and screwed with his concentration completely.

Ignoring this attraction was growing old fast. He couldn't do it. Couldn't spend the next thirty days working alongside her without going insane and taking enough cold showers to contribute to Melbourne's water shortage.

There was only so much curtailing a guy could take.

'Sapphire?'

She took an eternity to glance up, and when she did she was worrying her bottom lip with her top teeth. 'Yeah?'

'I think I should go.'

Schmuck that he was, he gave her one last out. If she agreed, he'd bolt—make that hobble—out of here. It was his final concession to the reformed him. One last attempt to do the right thing before he went frigging insane with wanting her and took whatever he could get.

He'd leave if she asked and make sure all their future meetings took place within office hours in an office environment. There was only so much temptation a guy could take.

He had no idea how long they stood there, the silence taut and expectant.

He could hear a clock ticking somewhere behind him, the

dripping of a faulty tap, and eventually the soft, wistful sigh of a woman as confused as him.

'Why?'

One word. That was all she uttered. It was enough.

He stalked towards her, even now expecting her to back-track, to make some flimsy excuse and turf him out on his ass.

Instead she stood ramrod straight, head tilted, unwavering stare defiant.

Lord, he wanted her. Wanted her with the kind of consuming lust that could make a man forget his name.

This thing between them went beyond a teenage fantasy, went beyond the basic craving for sensational sex. He saw something in her that called to him on some base level that defied logic. He couldn't label it—didn't want to. What he did want was her. Naked. Hot. Wet.

He stopped a foot in front of her, close enough to hear her sharp intake of breath, too damn far away when he wanted her body plastered against his.

'If I stay, it won't be for food.'

'Food can be overrated.' Her lips curved into a smug smile, sexy as hell. The kind of smile to give a guy depraved thoughts. 'So why *are* you staying?'

'You need me to spell it out?'

'I'd rather you show me—'

He claimed her mouth in a brutal kiss. No thought for sweet seduction or taking it slow. No thought beyond the incessant pounding in his head urging him to be inside her *now*.

She matched him, grabbing his shirt lapels, yanking him closer so that their bodies melded in a fusion of heat.

And it still wasn't enough.

He changed the pressure, his mouth sliding over hers in slow, tantalising sweeps, and she moaned, straining towards him.

With a tenuous hold on his self-control he grabbed her butt and hoisted her onto the breakfast bar—his turn to groan when his hard-on settled between her open legs. Her heat penetrated the clothing barriers between them and he wanted in.

She closed her eyes and arched into him, her abandonment so at odds with her usual reserve. He would come way too soon.

When her hips involuntarily moved, rubbing against him, he bit back an expletive. One that described what they were about to do.

If they had protection.

'Do you have condoms?'

Her eyes snapped open, incredibly blue amid the pink blush stealing into her cheeks. 'No. Don't you?'

He shook his head and cursed again. Cursed his stupidity in starting something he couldn't finish. Cursed his new lifestyle choices. Cursed the same impulses of the past that had got him here—frustrated as hell.

'You think Ruby would have any stocked in the bathroom?'

Sapphire frowned. 'Nope. She cleaned all her stuff out.'

For the first time in a long time he was at a loss for words. This was awkward. Rampaging lust was fine in the heat of the moment, but now…

'Though I guess we could double check?'

Her tone held a hint of devilry. He liked it. It meant she hadn't retreated or gone brusque on him. It also meant she might be up for other stuff if latex couldn't be found.

She snagged his hand and tugged him into the bathroom—surprisingly large compared with the rest of the apartment.

It had a glass-enclosed shower, a marble tub big enough for two and a floor-to-ceiling mirror with distinct possibilities.

She released his hand long enough to rummage through three drawers and a cabinet under the sink. He would have laughed at her frantic search if he weren't practically crippled from wanting her so badly.

When she straightened the disappointment in her eyes vindicated what he was about to do.

'Doesn't matter.'

Her mouth down-turned. 'Yeah, it does. I don't do unprotected sex.'

'Neither do I.' He reached out and touched her collarbone, then let his fingertip trail downward, around one breast, then the other, in slow concentric circles, until she sagged against the vanity. 'But there's loads we can do without the grand finale.'

Her eyes lit up as she registered the meaning behind his words and before he could say anything she'd whipped off her tee-shirt, giving him an eyeful of demi-cup black satin and pushed-up cleavage.

'Well, I guess that answers my next question—whether you'd be up for it or not.'

In response she reached for his zipper, tugged it down and slid her hand inside.

He gritted his teeth as she stroked him through the cotton of his boxers, until she reached the tip and he damn near exploded.

'Turn around.'

Her hand stilled at his command and her eyes widened, but he didn't see fear. He saw excitement and heat and yearning. Major turn on.

He missed her touch when she eased her hand out of his pants and swivelled towards the mirror but this would be worth the wait.

He wanted to watch her come.

He wanted to watch her watch him.

With surprisingly steady hands he popped the snap on her jeans, unzipped her and slid the denim down to midthigh-level.

Man, she was wearing a thong. Black satin. Same as the bra. He liked black. Some would say it matched his soul, but he didn't agree.

Right about now his soul was red. Fire-engine red. Crimson. The colour of passion and sin and debauchery. Maybe he'd buy her red lingerie for next time.

Her gaze was riveted to his hands as he hooked his thumbs into the elastic riding low on her hips and tugged, revealing her to him.

That expletive spilled from his lips again as he pressed against her—a gentle pressure that had her head falling back to rest on his shoulder.

But she didn't stop staring at his hand as he slid a finger between her slick folds, circling her, her wet heat driving him slowly but surely insane.

'Do you trust me?'

'I'm watching you pleasure me. What do you think?'

He grinned. Even now she was feisty. He liked it.

'Okay, then.'

He made quick work of tugging down his pants and boxers, biting back another curse when his hard-on made contact with her butt.

'Spread your legs a fraction,' he said, and slid between them when she did. The exquisite contact of his shaft with her moist heat almost undid him.

Amazingly, she didn't stop him or ask questions. She trusted him not to enter her and that knowledge, after all he'd been through over the last year, turned him on more than anything she could have said or done.

'Watch.'

He pushed forward, his erection fully between her legs, and she gasped as she saw him appear just beneath his hand.

'Keep watching.'

And she did, as he slid in and out between her legs, mimicking what he'd give anything to be doing deep inside her now.

As his finger picked up the tempo she started moving, her hips pushing back against him, urging him to go faster.

So he did. The torturous friction was building. Peaking. Crescendoing.

She arched a second before she screamed, riding his hand as he'd have liked to be riding her.

He eased away, shocked by the intensity of her orgasm, and even more suprised when she dropped to her knees.

'What are you doing—?'

'If you have to ask, you're not as good at all this as I thought.'

He would have laughed if she hadn't taken him into her mouth. All the way.

It was his turn to watch, but he didn't know where to look. At his fantasy come to life or in the mirror, where what she was doing was reflected back to him in eye-popping erotic detail.

He settled for watching her—the golden sheen of her hair beneath the bathroom lights, her lips surrounding him.

Then she started using her tongue and he lost it. He'd been close when she came, and all it took was three sweeps of her tongue around the tip

His orgasm ripped through him with the force of an explosion and he swore loudly.

As residual shudders of pleasure rippled through him he held out his hands to help her stand.

She ignored them, pulling up her jeans as she ducked down to the sink.

Uh-oh.

He made himself decent, waiting for her to finish and look at him. The tap eased to a drip, she used a handtowel, still didn't glance up.

'Look at me.'

After a few moments her reluctant gaze met his.

'Don't go having second thoughts now.' He snagged her hands, grateful she didn't pull away this time. 'What we just did blew my mind.'

Relief eased her drawn-together brows. 'You're inventive. I'll say that for you.'

He laughed, and thankfully she joined in. He liked that she hadn't clammed up on him or gone distant. He would have hated that.

'But for the record—next time I'm bringing a box.'

'To stand on?'

'Of condoms.' Buoyed by her sense of humour, he pulled her close, enveloping her in his arms with his chin resting on her head. 'Guess I should be grateful you didn't say there won't be a next time.'

She nuzzled his neck in response, and if it wasn't the damndest thing he was ready to go again. 'There'll be a next time. Count on it.'

He was. What he wasn't counting on was the dazed anticipation in his eyes as he stared at his reflection.

For a guy used to being in total control, a guy who liked his sex without commitment, a guy wary of anything more, he looked like a guy in way over his head.

CHAPTER FIVE

SAPPHIE SHOWERED AND brushed her teeth the next morning without looking in the mirror.

She couldn't. Not unless she wanted to go into meltdown.

The stupid thing was, she'd expected not to sleep last night—to be so wound up with analysing and second-guessing she couldn't—but the oddest thing had happened.

She'd had her first full night's sleep for months. Heck, for years.

And she owed it to Patrick.

Great, even thinking his name made her flush in remembrance.

What they'd done in this bathroom… Who would have thought having pseudo-sex could be so steamy?

She might not be super-experienced in that department—being a workaholic meant she could count the number of guys she'd thought hot enough to sleep with on one hand—but what she'd done with Patrick…

Wow. Simply *wow*.

And she still wanted him as badly this morning.

Her theory last night—that an orgasm might take the edge off her craziness and let her concentrate on working alongside him without the desperation to tear his clothes off—hadn't worked. It had backfired in a big way.

Now she wanted more. So much more. Both of them naked and sweaty. Going the whole way.

Stupid theories.

She should have ordered the take-out, made small talk, and let him walk out of here.

But the way he'd been looking at her... There was only so much willpower a girl could draw on.

Thankfully, it had been okay afterwards. They'd glossed over potential awkwardness, and he'd left after she'd pleaded tiredness and a need to prep for work tomorrow. Today. When she'd be seeing him again in less than an hour. Which meant she needed to apply make-up. Now.

With a groan she dragged herself back into the bathroom, took a deep breath and stared at her reflection.

Still the same tired old face, but there was a new glint in her eyes. A glint she didn't like. A glint that signalled a little bit of lust and a lot of crazy.

She blinked, hoping it would vanish.

Nope, still there. Lord only knew what Patrick would make of that glint.

She tried to concentrate on applying foundation, mascara, eyeshadow and lip gloss, she really did, but every time she focussed on the mirror a snippet of last night would flash into her head.

Courtesy of her shaky hands she'd gone through two applicators and a mascara wand already, and she resembled a clown.

Muttering a few choice curses under her breath, she gathered up her make-up and stalked towards the bedroom. The light might be crappy in there, and her clown face could worsen, but she'd take the risk. She'd rather apply make-up in the tiny oval mirror tacked onto the wardrobe door than use the bathroom one.

Maybe she could call a glazier today and have him remove it?

Then again, Patrick had promised to bring a box of condoms next time, and her newly discovered inner vixen really had had a lot of fun watching…

Realistically, she shouldn't want a repeat. Sex with Patrick would be phenomenal but wrong. A giant complication just waiting to happen.

But she'd felt so good last night—*alive* in a way she hadn't in a long time.

The chronic fatigue syndrome symptoms had drained her mentally, emotionally and physically, particularly the latter, and it was her need to reassert her fitness that was driving her to follow through with Patrick.

Nothing like a sex-a-thon to give a girl a workout.

Okay, so she was making light of the situation, probably making excuses to go through with it too, but Patrick had made her feel sensational last night and she wanted to feel that good again.

The post-orgasmic endorphins had lasted a long time after he'd left, and for the first time in ages she'd had the energy to unpack the rest of her cases, clean the kitchen and rearrange her DVDs and books.

She'd bounced around the apartment, humming eighties tunes and shimmying between cleaning, feeling so good she could have run a marathon.

How long since she'd felt that invincible?

Logically, sex with Patrick might be a disaster. Physically? She'd help him haul that box of condoms over pronto.

Patrick needed neutral. A neutral playing field where he could work alongside Sapphire without the constant urge to rip her clothes off.

Last night had only worsened his lust for her. A small part of him had hoped it would ease. *Yeah, right.*

He should have known better than to believe his delusional self-talk that a quickie with Sapphire would soothe him.

A guy didn't do what he had done with Sapphire last night

and *get it out of his system*. Not to mention the added tension of knowing she was up for more. A whole box-worth more.

He didn't get it. It wasn't as if he'd been hung up on her in the past. He'd enjoyed baiting her at school, made it his mission to get a rise out of her because he'd wanted to ruffle her uptight exterior. Sure, he'd had the odd fantasy about her—what teenage guy hadn't?

Sapphire was an attractive woman now. It figured that he'd want to have sex with her. The part he hadn't figured out was why it was pounding through his brain until it was all he could think about.

He couldn't afford distractions—not with so much at stake. But the thought of using a box-worth of condoms pleasuring Sapphire Seaborn couldn't be denied, and he'd damn well better get control of his libido before he botched this business opportunity before it had begun.

'Hey, Rick, the models are ready.'

Patrick glanced up at his right-hand man and best bud, Serge. Though they'd ripped a path through Europe's party scene together when Patrick had needed the distraction, while Serge continued to live the high life Patrick now opted for more sedate pursuits: like making his fashion house dreams come true.

They'd grown apart over the years but Serge was still a good manager, and it helped having someone he could trust on his side. He couldn't say that about many people.

'Thanks, but Sapphire's not here yet. Give us five.'

'No worries.' Serge spoke into a bluetooth clipped near his right ear before slipping onto the chair next to him. 'What's up?'

Great. Just what he needed. Serge's legendary interrogation. He had no intention of telling anyone about Sapphire—not when they'd be working together. But he and Serge had told tall tales over beers too many times to count, and the guy could read him like the latest bestseller.

'Not much.' Patrick pointed towards the stack of documents in front of him. 'This is taking up all my time.'

'Bull.'

Patrick sat back, folded his arms and feigned ignorance. He only succeeded in making Serge laugh.

'Work never fazes you. You took on that spring showing in Paris and hit it out of the ballpark.' Serge tilted his head to one side, studying him. 'Nah, this isn't about work. This is about a chick.'

Patrick didn't want to discuss Sapphire with Serge but he hated dishonesty.

'That Paris gig? What we're doing here has to nail that a hundred times over and you know it.'

Serge smirked. 'I also know whoever this chick is, she must be special for you to be this rattled.'

Thankfully Sapphire's arrival put paid to any further ribbing from Serge but it disconcerted him in a whole other way.

She'd gone for masculine chic today: crisp white shirt, fitted ebony pinstripe pants suit, designer loafers, hair slicked back, dramatic make-up. It didn't detract from her femininity. He'd seen exactly how womanly she could be last night.

What her mouth had done to him…

His gaze found its way to her lips—their sheen, their fullness—and he instantly hardened.

He heard Serge's hissed breath of surprise as she strode towards them and he knew the feeling. When Sapphire Seaborn walked towards a man he wanted to meet her halfway.

'She's a stunner,' Serge muttered under his breath, earning a glare from Patrick that probably increased his friend's speculation.

Let Serge think what he liked. He wasn't getting one snippet of information about Patrick's private life here in Melbourne. Patrick had moved on from the carousing of the past and intended focussing on things that mattered. Namely:

wowing Fashion Week. And bedding Sapphire. Not necessarily in that order.

She barely glanced at him when she reached them, focussing a dazzling smile on Serge instead. 'Hi. Sapphire Seaborn.'

Serge grinned like the predatory male he was and snagged her hand, raising it to his lips. 'The pleasure's all mine, *mademoiselle*.'

When Serge kissed her hand, Patrick had to clench his to stop from slugging him.

'You're French?'

Serge nodded and, luckily for him, released her hand. *'Oui.'*

'He's as Anglicised as you and I,' Patrick said, shooting him a frown. 'Only uses the accent to win friends and influence women.'

'It's charming.'

Figured. What was it with females and European accents?

'Serge was just leaving to organise the models for a quick demo if you're ready?'

Sapphire finally looked at him, her gaze imperious, the tilt of her head snooty. 'Sure, let's get started.'

She made it sound as if he'd chastised her unnecessarily, when in fact he'd wanted to get rid of his leery friend pronto.

'Au revoir, Sapphire.' Serge gave a formal little bow and Patrick gritted his teeth. 'We will meet again.'

'No doubt.'

If her smile had been dazzling before, she notched it up a level now. What red-blooded guy stood a chance?

Patrick mentally counted to ten, slowly, waiting until Serge had left the room.

'Don't flirt with Serge. It only encourages him,' he said, trying to sound casual and failing miserably if her inverted eyebrow and smirk were any indication.

'I was being polite, not flirting, but thanks for the advice.'

She slid onto a seat and patted the one next to him. 'Now, why don't you sit so we can talk business?'

Fan-frigging-tastic. He'd been mulling over how to approach this first meeting post-bathroom and she'd waltzed in here as if nothing had happened, gaining the upper hand and commandeering the conversation.

Patrick didn't like losing control. Bad things happened. Things he'd never risk happening again.

'Talking business is fine,' he said, sitting next to her and deliberately leaning into her personal space. 'For now.'

The faintest stain of pink on her cheeks was the only indication that he'd scored a hit. She didn't respond, taking her sweet time slipping a slimline laptop out of her satchel and setting it up, laying a blank notepad and pen next to it.

Only then did she swivel in her seat to face him, her imperious mask firmly in place. 'Don't you think it's a tad unprofessional, bringing up our social activities in the workplace?'

Her directness impressed him. But the resumption of her haughtiness, not so much. Hadn't she learned by now that the snootier she acted, the harder he worked to rile her?

'Social activities?' He lowered his voice to barely above a whisper, his lips almost brushing her ear. 'Why don't we call it what it is? Good old-fashioned f—'

'Keep that up and there won't be any *socialising* of any kind,' she said, shoving him away, her tone frosty.

'You haven't changed a bit,' he said, chuckling at her rigid shoulders and ramrod spine as she determinedly stared at her laptop screen. 'You always needed to have the last word during our Biology assignments too.'

'I did not.' She shot him a death glare.

'Yeah, you did. And it's just as cute now.' He smiled, waiting for her to glance his way.

He didn't have to wait long. She blew out an exasperated breath before angling her chair towards him.

'Okay, the thing is this: I'm confident in the business arena.

Invincible. But what happened last night threw me, and focussing on work is the only way I can handle this without...'

'What?'

'Without losing it,' she said softly, her wide-eyed baby-blues imploring him to listen. 'Aren't you just the tiniest bit uncomfortable?'

He shrugged. 'Sure, but honestly? That ice princess act you had down pat in Biology only made me want to taunt you more. And when I first rocked up in Melbourne it looked like nothing had changed. Then last night...' He shook his head, still blown away by the erotic memories that had filtered across his consciousness ever since. 'I got a glimpse of how hot you are beneath the ice and it's a major turn-on. Last night was great. Stupendous, in fact. And a great prelude to going the whole way. So I'm not going to make excuses for it or apologise or act recalcitrant.' He pinned her with a direct stare. 'For the fact is I'd do it again right now, right here.'

Her frosty façade melted a little as her mouth curved at the corners. 'I've always wanted to do it on a desk.'

'Duly noted.' He trailed a fingertip across the back of her hand where it rested on her lap. 'For the record, mine's padded.'

'No, it's not. It's bevelled glass.'

He winked. 'I'll make sure to bring a blanket next time we meet in my office.'

She waggled her finger at him. 'Didn't I just say we should keep business and social stuff separate?'

'Yeah, but that doesn't mean I agree with it.'

She huffed out an exasperated breath—something she'd done often when they'd been studying. 'You know we have to talk about what happened last night, right?'

They did? From where he was sitting, he'd rather be doing much more than talking. Like finishing what they'd started last night, with him deep within her this time around.

'Talk is overrated.'

'Spoken like a true male,' she said drily, jabbing him in the chest. 'We need boundaries, that sort of thing.'

'We need a desk with our name written all over it,' he said, *sotto voce*, earning a delightfully unassuming, tempting pout for his trouble.

'You're the same infuriating, annoying, over-confident—'

'And you're the same subtly sexy, smart, amazing woman,' he said, meaning it.

He'd met some incredible women around the world, had enjoyed every moment of his bachelor life, but it hadn't been until he'd arrived back in Melbourne and strutted into Seaborns that he'd remembered Sapphire had a certain something that elevated her among other females.

He couldn't explain what it was, but the hint of vulnerability underlying her usual toughness appealed on a deeper level he rarely acknowledged.

And that meant he had to focus on one thing only. Sex. No time or inclination to discover where her newfound softness had come from or to delve beyond the obvious: they were two people with a serious sexual attraction that would combust if last night's prelude was any indication.

And he couldn't wait for the main event.

Her mouth opened, closed. Her loss of words was cute. A rarity. He took full advantage.

'I meant what I said.' He snagged her hand beneath the table and she let him. 'I had no idea you were so hot in high school—' She pursed her lips in disapproval and he rushed on '—which is probably a good thing, as I would've made you fail Biology. But seeing how into it you were last night, us hooking up, major turn-on. Fantasy stuff.'

He must have said the right thing, because she turned her hand over and intertwined her fingers with his. 'You drove me nuts in high school, teasing me and mucking around with your slackass attitude.'

'Surely that kiss on graduation night redeemed me slightly?

She winced. 'Another thing I'd rather not talk about.'

'Yeah, I kinda got that impression when you didn't return my calls.'

Her fingers convulsed for a second. 'I was mortified.'

'Why? Because your date was a drunken dumbass?'

She shook her head, dislodging a few strands from her slicked back do. Mussing the severity of that product-drenched hair added to her vulnerability.

'No, I was embarrassed because I'd treated you badly yet you didn't hesitate in stepping in to help me out of a rough spot.'

He saw genuine regret in the reluctant gaze that met his, and he didn't like his answering zap of emotion.

Who cared what her motivations had been back then? He wanted her in his bed now. That was all that mattered. No room for emotions whatsoever.

'Hey, I liked the putdowns and the cutting remarks. It spurred me on to tease you harder.'

'That's what the kiss was about, wasn't it?'

She'd lost him.

'Huh?'

'I thought you kissed me out of pity.'

She said it so softly he strained forward to hear it.

'What the—?'

'I thought you felt sorry for me after Mick ditched me at the dance,' she said, bolder this time, daring him to disagree. 'You teased me during the drive about my lousy taste in dates, said maybe it was my dress or my hair or my corsage that drove him away, then we got home and you kissed me and I thought it was a big joke—you taking your usual taunts that one step further.'

He swore.

'You thought I was that shallow?'

'That's the only side of you I ever saw,' she said, as if that made it better.

It didn't. There was a reason he'd acted that way, why he'd only shown the world a certain side, but he couldn't tell her. He'd divulged enough truths for one day.

'Well, sweetheart, here's a tip. When a guy kisses a girl it isn't out of pity. It's usually driven by hormones.'

He shrugged, trying to make light of the situation before he blabbed about why he'd really kissed her that night. It wouldn't help to admit he had felt sorry for her, that he'd kissed her as a distraction to prevent tears. She'd slug him for sure. Or worse, not follow through on the promise of sensational sex.

So he was a guy? Sue him.

'And here's a heads up. My motivation for kissing you back then is irrelevant. Because all that matters now is I sure as hell want you. *Right now,* if I had my way.' He tugged on her hand and she leaned in close. 'I'd clear this table, hoist you onto it, and have you out of those pants in two seconds flat.'

Her eyes widened, locked on his. Thankfully she'd lost the injured lamb look. He could handle her cool and controlled. He didn't do her insecure side well. It unnerved him, seeing the woman who'd verbally fended off his barbs and then some all soft and susceptible.

It made him *feel* stuff he didn't want to, so he regained control the only way he knew how.

'I'd spread your legs, start at your right knee and kiss my way upward. Nipping your inner thigh…gentle bites.'

Her sharp intake of breath spurred him on.

'I'd tease my way along your hip, across your belly to the other side, where I'd kiss you all the way down. Hot, openmouthed kisses, until you were squirming for me.' He locked gazes with her. 'Begging for it.'

She groaned.

He knew the feeling.

'Keep going,' she said, squirming in her seat.

'Then I'd lick my way up your thigh until I could hardly

control myself. But I'd taste you, circling you with my tongue, sucking you into my mouth until you came—'

'Patrick, please…'

He released her hand in her lap and edged over, cupping her mound. She cursed, the word spilling from her lips as much of a turn-on as her reaction to him here in the boardroom.

The fact she was letting him do this to her here, with the risk of anyone walking in, heightened the pleasure.

'Yeah, I'd love to be doing that to you right now, but this will have to suffice.'

He pushed the heel of his hand into her and she ground against it. It took several small, circular undulations of for her to come, her fingers digging into his thigh while she lifted off the chair slightly.

They never broke eye contact the entire time, so he saw everything. Her need, her passion, her release.

And it humbled him in a way he'd never dreamed possible.

If he'd thought he was in over his head last night, her response to him now made him feel like a drowning man without a chance of being saved.

The door creaked open and they sprang apart. She muttered underneath her breath: he tried to act as if wanting to tear this woman's clothes off every time he saw her wasn't all that unusual.

Sex…nothing more, nothing less. Maybe if he mentally recited it often enough he'd believe it.

He shot her a glance but she stared straight ahead, fixed on the models strutting through the room in preliminary designs, the pinkness of her cheeks the only giveaway sign that she wasn't the same über-cool princess he remembered.

Fine, let them concentrate on business for now, but when they'd wrapped up here they needed to sort out where and when they were going to get this *thing* out of their system— for he had a feeling he wouldn't be functioning on any useful level until he did.

* * *

Sapphie had learned from a young age to shield her real feelings.

The expectations associated with being the eldest child, the one with highest grades, the responsible one, had pretty much ensured she was under scrutiny as heir apparent to run Seaborns from the time she hit high school.

Maybe even before, considering her mum had spent every Saturday afternoon poring over the company's finances and making Sapphie sit next to her.

When kids her age had been riding their scooters or playing netball on the weekend, she'd been tagging along on buying expeditions, or scouting the opposition, or hanging around at fancy tea parties, listening to her mum talk shop.

Sure, she'd learned to love Seaborns, and had strived to gain great grades to enter her chosen Economics and Management degree, but over the years it had become ingrained to maintain a calm outer persona. To pretend everything was right with the world. When in fact she'd had bad hair days and hated the school bully and crushed on the football captain.

That persona would serve her well now, when she had to sit next to Patrick during a preview and pretend he hadn't just rocked her world again.

What he'd done... What she'd let him do...

Her fingers convulsed, digging into her thighs. She'd never been wild or wanton. Maybe that was her problem. When an experienced playboy like Patrick glanced sideways at her she was ready to jump him.

She blamed Ruby and all that talk of getting laid. Sure, it had been a while since she'd been with a guy, but she hadn't really been interested, what with the fatigue.

Ironic that coming back to work and throwing herself into this campaign was all about physically proving she could handle leading Seaborns, but what if there was a better way to test her endurance? Or at least a more fun way?

For she had little doubt sex with Patrick would involve an aerobic capacity workout to push her to the limit.

As if sensing her wicked, wayward thoughts he cast her a glance, which she deftly deflected by pretending to concentrate on the models strutting into the room.

Thankfully he returned to muttering into his smartphone, dictating changes and minor adjustments on the gowns to follow up later: hem too low here, stray seam there. He was so focussed, so tuned in to his work, she couldn't help but stare a little.

He'd surprised her. She'd wondered if he could pull off his mega idea for old-world Hollywood glamour, and by the looks of the early designs he'd come through in a big way.

It pained her to admit, even to herself, that she'd doubted him. But she had, and now she was going to have to eat her words.

How could the guy who'd laughed his way through school before absconding to Paris be responsible for these exquisite designs?

She glanced at the models, poised in a holding pattern on a makeshift runway, stunned anew by the colours and gowns before her eyes.

A riot of rich hues: deep crimson, emerald, peacock-blue. Lush satins, shimmering silks. Strapless evening gowns. Timeless cocktail frocks. Curves and class. Absolutely stunning.

Patrick might not have personally drawn the designs, but he'd come up with the concept, had supervised the designers night and day to get them to this point.

Not only did the guy have a sound business head, he had creativity to burn.

And not just for this fashion show.

She resisted the urge to squirm in her seat—and tried to ignore the occasional brush of his shoulder against hers or the touch of his thigh pressing close as he leaned over to point out a minor detail. Perfectly innocuous actions that shouldn't have made her burn but she did. For him. With an unrelenting heat that sparked every time he touched her and shot off at tangents throughout her body, zapping and scalding and corroding her resistance slowly but surely.

This wasn't good.

Their bathroom interlude should have taken the edge off her sudden interest in seeing him naked.

Instead it had put her on some heightened awareness where having him near sent her pheromones into overdrive.

The preview concluded way too quickly. Serge departed and the models filed out after him, leaving her rueing the approaching time where she'd have to do some fast thinking, fast talking, or both.

She'd had an orgasm.

In Fourde Fashion's boardroom.

With an unlocked door.

Seconds before people had come traipsing in.

It had been phenomenal, but the fact she was becoming like him—reckless, live in the moment—was not good.

That might have been one of her goals after leaving Tenang—to make the most of every second and not dwell on things she couldn't change—but now she had Patrick urging her, how far would she go to test her newfound strength?

Pushing it physically was one thing, but seeing how far she could push with Patrick...

Danger with a capital D.

For sex with a guy like him could become addictive, and she had no intention of getting hooked.

'Thoughts?'

He really didn't want to know.

By the amused glint in his eyes, maybe he did.

She took a deep breath and pushed her notepad towards him. 'On what you've done? Amazing. Here are a few things I jotted down to capitalise on the theme you're going for.'

He sped read her dot-point list, nodding thoughtfully, pen tapping against the pad, so absorbed in business that she wondered if she'd dreamt the whole dirty-talk orgasm incident.

'Great pick-ups. I'll get onto Serge right away to get the designers to incorporate.'

He glanced up and her heart leapt.

'Sure Ruby's the only creative genius in your family?' He pointed at the list. 'These are insightful suggestions.'

Chuffed by his praise, she shrugged. 'This coming from the guy who has single-handedly come up with an amazing concept and is seeing it through to the most glorious designs I've ever seen.'

He winked. 'Flattery will get you everywhere.'

That was what she was afraid of.

Now was the time she had to lay down the law about mixing business with pleasure, about setting boundaries. But with her body still humming and her mind still reeling at how sexual he made her feel, maybe now wasn't the best time.

He touched her arm, the barest brush of his fingertips against her skin, and she jumped.

'Your reaction just answered my next question.'

'What's that?'

'That until we get this thing out of our systems are we going to be useless working together?'

She should disagree. Should give him a spiel about her ability to remain professional and focussed at all times.

Totally hypocritical, considering she'd almost screamed his name less than thirty minutes ago.

'What do you suggest?'

'Damned if I know.' He pinched the bridge of his nose. It did little to clear the frown above it. 'We have three weeks left 'til Fashion Week, so the next seven days are crucial in finalising the designs and incorporating changes.'

No argument there.

'That means we both need to work our butts off without interruptions.' He sent her a pointed glare. 'Or distractions.'

'Hey, I'm not the one going around...' She trailed off, unwilling to articulate exactly what he'd been doing to her. 'So you're saying we work apart?'

Was that even feasible with the workload they had?

He nodded, and while her head said this was the perfect solution, her body wailed a loud, resounding *nooooo!*

'We talk on the phone, e-mail, Skype. But this?' He gestured to the limited space between them. 'Too distracting when I can't keep my hands off you.'

His declaration soothed her wailing body somewhat.

'But some time in the future, when the campaign is done...' He snagged a tendril curling around her ear and wound it slowly around his finger, caressing the top of her ear, tracing its shape, sending a shiver of longing vibrating downwards. 'We play.'

How two words could hold so much promise she'd never know.

'Define play.'

His mouth eased into a breath-stealing grin. 'You and me. "Do not Disturb" sign. And that box I promised you. Maybe two.'

Her body gave a betraying howl of longing.

'Your stamina's that good?'

'You bet.' He leaned close, his lips grazing her cheek, and she clamped down on the urge to turn her head a fraction and ram her mouth against his. 'And I can't wait to prove it.'

Oh, boy.

'Sound doable?'

She—it—was extremely doable.

'Sure.' She nodded, her insides trembling with need, as she gathered up her work paraphernalia.

'Sapphire?'

She couldn't stop, for if she did she'd never make it out of here without flinging herself at him.

'Yeah?' she mumbled, trying to stuff her laptop into her bag with limited success—until she realised she was trying to force it into her handbag.

'You know time apart will feed my hunger for you?'

She gulped.

If they were this turned on now, imagine what time apart would do?

'And while we focus on business this next week it doesn't rule out phone sex.'

A ripple of pleasure spread through her at the thought.

'I've never done phone sex,' she said, sounding like an inexperienced neophyte but not caring. She had a feeling this guy would be teaching her a plethora of unspoken delights.

'Then this is going to be fun.'

He brushed a kiss across her lips and she let him, lingering a few seconds longer than necessary, aware it would be their last physical contact for a long seven days.

When the need to linger became a driving need to straddle him, she yanked away and grabbed her stuff.

She strode for the door, desperate to put some distance between them. With her hand on the handle and a safe space between them, she said, 'Patrick?'

'Yeah?'

Her only consolation was that he looked half as dazed as she was.

'Better make that three boxes.'

CHAPTER SIX

SAPPHIE LASTED A whole three days without succumbing to the temptation of seeing Patrick's face.

Then he sent her a text, citing an urgent Skype meeting, and she caved.

Purely business, of course. And the fact she spent ten minutes primping in front of a mirror? It was the usual routine she'd do before any work meeting.

The part where her palms grew clammy as she swiped on mascara and scrubbed off her lippy twice before settling on the perfect shade was pure feminine preening.

She had four more days before he made good on his promise. Just the two of them and a decadent weekend. With boxes.

She'd been a smart-ass, taunting him at the conclusion of their last face-to-face meeting, but deep down she was a quivering mess of confusion and nerves and lust. The kind of lust she'd never experienced. The kind of lust guaranteed to turn her into a fool.

She didn't suffer fools lightly, and respected hard work and dedication in comparison with deceitful women who faked helplessness in order to score points with men. The type of women Patrick usually hung out with if the internet was anything to go by.

It had been a stupid, spur-of-the moment decision to check out his more recent past, spurred by two glasses of Chardonnay and a rampant curiosity.

It had been the end of a long eighteen-hour day—the day after she'd seen him; a day in which she'd determinedly buried herself in work to erase the lingering memory of his touch, and her response.

The wine had helped her wind down but it hadn't taken the edge off her curiosity and she'd succumbed to temptation.

The internet had been enlightening, to say the least, and had provided her with a plethora of images and articles. Usually depicting Patrick with a stunning supermodel on his arm, laughing into the camera, with a different country landscape in the background. From Santorini to Monte Carlo, Nice to Barcelona, Patrick was there, partying his way through Europe.

She'd given up after the tenth page. The endless hits had been rather depressing.

He'd lived such an exciting life amid glamorous people while she'd spent the last ten years devoting hers to Seaborns.

She didn't regret a single moment—discounting the last year when she'd been an idiot in shouldering the burden alone—and still experienced a thrill when she walked into their amazing showroom. But seeing pictorial evidence of Patrick's lifestyle reinforced what she'd always felt around him: gauche, prim, floundering a little.

And envious. She'd always been a tad envious of his ability to charm people, his ease to cruise through life without a care in the world, his natural exuberance that made everyone around him smile.

If anything, those images had reinforced what she already knew deep down: that Patrick was way different and always had been. Back in high school he'd annoyed her, so what had changed now? He was still brash and cocky and charming, and had waltzed into this new Fourde Fashion with the ease of a practised CEO.

As far as she could tell from her research he'd been a minion in Paris, so this position was a massive boost up the corporate ladder for him. From what she'd been able to find of his professional life, that was. There'd been a glut of social stuff and pics, and *nada* on his work. She'd found it odd but had been too depressed by the gorgeous glamazons on his arm in every photo to worry about it.

And that exacerbated her annoyance—the fact he'd probably been handed this job on a silver platter and would rock it because he had the backing of his family name.

The irony wasn't lost on her: people would say the same about her and Seaborns. But there was a difference. She'd been groomed from a young age to take over, had acted in accordance because of it. Had made sacrifices, had never lost sight of the end goal, had strived to be the best leader this jewellery company had ever seen.

Could Patrick say the same? Doubtful.

For a guy who'd spent his final year doodling and folding origami figures with his study notes he'd come a long way.

And judging by this current show he was nailing it too.

Admiration tempered her annoyance at his glib, charmed life. The guy might have skived off during that final year at high school but he was putting in the hard yards now.

And she admired hard work. She understood it. What she didn't understand was her undeniable, clamouring attraction to him.

She felt *good* around him, in a way she hadn't in a long time. Her skin tingled, her blood pounded and she felt *alive*.

Proving she could physically handle her role as Seaborns' boss was one thing, but handling whatever Patrick dished out took her recovery to a whole other level.

Matching him sexually would push her out of her comfort zone, and it would take the edge off this insane lust she had for him.

Most importantly, it would prove to herself she was whole again.

That had been the worst part of her enforced rest at Tenang—the insidious self-doubts that would creep up on her at inopportune moments and make her wonder if she had what it took to continue leading Seaborns.

For someone who'd loved being the face of the company, who'd attended posh soirées and glamorous events and talked up Seaborn's fabulous jewellery every chance she got, during her recovery she'd wondered if she'd ever find that kind of energy again.

Sure, she'd improved, but every time she yawned or had a twinge in her muscles or a minor headache from spending too long at the computer, she experienced a fleeting panic that she could suffer a relapse.

Being with Patrick, having him desire her, made her feel physically thriving, and that, more than anything, silenced her doubts in getting sexually involved with him.

Anything, or any*one*, that could make her feel on this constant high, as if she was invincible, was worth pursuing.

She remembered the way he'd looked at her those times he'd pleasured her, the way he'd been turned on, the way he devoured her with his eyes every time he thought she wasn't looking—and her body buzzed.

The endorphin release from Patrick's touch was much better than any workout.

But craving him this much…how had she morphed from a successful, confident businesswoman to this muddle of need?

His fault for being so darn appealing. Which raised the question: if she did throw herself into a dirty little fling with him, would her sensibilities return or would this crazy, out of control feeling intensify?

She couldn't afford the latter—needed to ensure Seaborns presented their best work at the Fashion Week show. A real quandary: indulge in a no-holds-barred fling with Patrick, feel utterly amazing and the best she had in ages. Or walk away from any further physical involvement and run the risk of going completely batty wanting him regardless.

She stuck her tongue out at her reflection. How had she ended up in this situation?

She didn't lust after guys—especially ones who'd driven her nuts in high school. She worked hard and worked out. That was the extent of her life.

Maybe that was half the problem?

Probably. Which was why a decadent weekend of raunchy sex could be just what the doctor ordered.

She chuckled, wondering what the physicians at Tenang would think about that as a treatment for CFS.

Though could she do it? Shuck off her business suit and become a sex-starved goddess for a weekend with Patrick?

As she settled in front of her PC and waited for Patrick's Skype call one thought reverberated through her head: *first time for everything.*

Patrick had worked his ass off the last three days. Pulled an all-nighter. Done the work of ten men. Supervised and brain-stormed and delegated.

Usually this manic pace gave him a buzz. In the past it had come from partying; these days it was from ensuring Fourde Fashion stayed ahead of competing European designers.

This time working like a maniac hadn't taken the edge off. Only one woman could do that and he couldn't wait to see her—even if it was only via a screen.

He didn't like how she'd got under his skin. Didn't like the anticipation making his palms clammy. She was a distraction he could ill afford but somehow, despite working his butt off, he couldn't stop thinking about her.

At least Skype was safe. A visual without the temptation of touching. And he'd been doing a lot of that, fantasising about touching her...

He'd half expected Sapphire not to respond to his call, but in a few seconds she appeared, her eyes wide and luminous, her cheeks pink, her lips glossed, and his gut tightened.

'Hey, gorgeous.'

'Hey.' A smile played around her lips but it didn't quite reach her eyes. 'What did you want to discuss tonight?'

'Business, of course.'

He had to stay focussed on business before he ignored his vow to stay away from her and drove like a maniac to her apartment.

Seeing her, even through a screen, wasn't such a smart idea after all. He should have stuck to e-mails.

'Good.' She nodded, as if his answer had allayed her fears of getting too personal. 'What did you think of those shots I e-mailed this morning?'

'Ruby's incredibly talented.' He held up a sketch. 'The embedded sapphire choker will look amazing with this evening gown. And the emerald dog collar will accentuate the showstopper perfectly.'

'Great.' Her shoulders relaxed a little but her studiously polite smile didn't slip. 'What about the yellow diamond set? Could it be used with the saffron sheath or the alabaster A-line?'

'Think we'll make that decision when the models wear the final pieces.'

'Timelines still on track?'

He nodded. 'Absolutely.'

'Good, because we've been working like maniacs over here.'

'Same here.' He slipped a finger between his tie and collar. 'I'm in danger of becoming a very dull boy.'

Her lips quirked into a coy smile. 'I doubt that.'

'I miss playing,' he said, knowing he shouldn't flirt but unable to stop.

'I never have time to.'

He heard the wistful undertone, well aware that if she were anything like she'd been in high school Sapphire would never take time out to play.

'Everyone should make time to play. It's healthy.'

'So I've been told,' she said, glancing away from the screen, fiddling with the neckline of her dress.

In that moment he knew exactly how to make her come out to play.

He locked fingers, stretched and settled them behind his head. 'Tell me what you're wearing.'

A cute little crease appeared between her brows. 'Pretty obvious, I would've thought. Ochre shift dress.'

'I meant what you're wearing beneath it.'

Her lips parted in a delightful O of surprise before she clamped them shut. 'We are *so* not having Skype sex.'

'Why not?'

'Because.' She darted a glance away from the screen. Probably trying to find something to cover the inbuilt camera. 'I don't see the point.'

'The point being it's fun to play. And if you're half as horny as me it might take the edge off.' He unlocked his hands and leaned towards the camera. 'Plus I love seeing you get off.'

A deep crimson flushed her cheeks.

'Come on, give a guy a little something to tide him over while he's working all-nighters.'

The tip of her tongue darted out to moisten her bottom lip before she said, 'I—I—haven't done this before. I'm not sure—'

'It's all about the fantasy, sweetheart.' He lowered his voice, knowing he needed to say the right thing or he'd lose her. 'There's no right or wrong way. Just do what feels good.'

She paused, worrying her bottom lip for a few indecisive seconds, before her chin tilted and he knew he had her.

'You tell anyone about this and you're a dead man.'

Victorious, he leaned back in his chair. 'Consider this a prelude to the real thing.'

She nodded, and a sweep of hair the colour of gold silk swished across one eye before she pushed it back impatiently.

'Let's try this again. Tell me what you're wearing.'

She inhaled and blew out a breath. 'Pale pink lace.'

'Bra and panties?'

'Thong,' she corrected, and his hard-on twitched.

'Sheer?'

'Yep.'

He cursed.

'Take off your thong.'

Her eyes widened. 'Patrick—'

'Do it,' he said, his voice thick with lust. 'And I want to see proof.'

'I'm not doing that—'

'Relax, just seeing the thong will do.' He grinned. 'For now.'

She huffed out a breath but he saw her wiggling, and in a few moments she waved the flimsiest excuse for underwear he'd ever seen in front of the camera.

'Satisfied?'

'Not by a long shot, babe, but we're getting there.'

He wondered how far he could push her and decided to go all the way.

'Now touch yourself.' He throbbed, and shifted in his chair. 'You're turned on, wet, and as you touch yourself I want you to imagine it's my tongue.'

She moaned, and it was the sweetest sound he'd ever heard via electronic medium.

'I'll do it,' she said, 'but only if you do it too.'

Kudos to his sexy Sapphire. She was a quick learner.

'Okay, but only because you asked so nicely.'

He unzipped and sprang free of his boxers, rigid and straining. As he wrapped his fingers around himself he closed his eyes, visualising the encounter he'd had with Sapphire in her bathroom. How her breasts had bounced as he'd thrust between her legs, how slick she'd been, how her face had looked as she came.

'Can you feel my mouth on you?' she said, and it was his turn to groan. 'Because I'm taking you in all the way as I'm touching myself.'

He wanted to open his eyes, to watch her face, but he knew if he did this would be over all too quickly.

'Tell me what you feel like,' he said, moving his hand, wishing it were hers.

'I'm so wet for you,' she murmured, giving a little pant of surprise. 'I think I'm going to come pretty soon.'

'That's good, because I was ready to blow the second I imagined your mouth around me.'

'Let's do this together, okay?'

He heard the vulnerability in her voice and his eyes snapped open. And, yeah, he immediately wished he'd kept them closed.

She had an incredibly rapt expression, filled with wonderment and excitement and awe, and it made him want to fling himself through the screen and cyberspace to sweep her into his arms.

Her wondrous gaze never left his. 'Patrick, I'm so close…'

'Come for me,' he said, his hand quickening as his muscles tightened in pre-release.

'Patrick…this feels…*oooh*…'

She came on a drawn-out keen and it was enough to push him over the edge.

His mind blanked as he blasted to outer space and back, despite the fact this had been a poor substitute for where he'd like to be.

'Patrick?'

'Hmm?'

'I have a newfound respect for Skype.'

'Good, because we're having another *business* meeting tomorrow night.'

* * *

Patrick was a glutton for punishment.

It was the only explanation for why he'd agreed to personally drop off the fabric swatches to Ruby at Seaborns.

Though it wasn't Ruby he was hoping to see and he knew it.

It had been two nights since his Skype session with Sapphire and while he hadn't contacted her since he couldn't stop thinking about her.

She invaded his every waking moment, and most sleeping ones too.

His vow not to be distracted by her during preparations for this show was not working out so great.

He didn't like feeling this...*confused*. Women always held some fascination, but in the past he'd been able to relegate them to his downtime without a problem. But Sapphire? Whether he was working, or at the gym burning off his frustration, she was there, in his mind, the echo of her pleasure reverberating in his ears until he couldn't think straight.

Turning up at Seaborns today was about proving to himself he wasn't enthralled. That he had a grip on this thing between them. That he wasn't such a schmuck he couldn't control his libido.

Then Sapphire opened the door and his blasé self-talk faded into oblivion.

'Thanks for dropping the swatches by,' she said, holding open the door and beckoning him in. 'Ruby's dying to match them to the latest batch of gems.'

'No worries,' he said, taking great care not to brush her as he entered.

One touch and he'd take her up against the nearest glass display case.

'Want a drink?'

He swallowed his first response, a resounding *no*, and nodded out of politeness. 'Sure, coffee would be great.'

'Through here.'

He followed her into a tiny kitchenette at the back of the showroom and immediately regretted his decision to stay, manners be damned. The room was no bigger than a box. A very tiny box that resulted in her light cinnamon peach perfume mingling with the coffee bean aroma and wrapping around him in a sweet, tempting blend.

While the percolator did its thing, she propped herself against the bench and he struggled not to stare at the teal silk wraparound dress that did incredible things to her body and highlighted the sparkle in her eyes.

'Can I see the swatches?'

He wanted to fling the fabric samples at her and make a run for it while he still could. For he knew without a doubt that if she took a step towards him he wouldn't be able to keep his hands off her.

'Yeah.'

He fished them out of his pocket and held the swatches at arm's length, earning an amused smile.

'For someone who was mighty forward the other night, I find your sudden reticence intriguing.'

'Just take the swatches,' he said, gritting his teeth against the urge to say more.

Such as what he'd like to do to her right here, right now, up against the tiny kitchen bench.

'You? Shy?' She reached out and rubbed a piece of crimson satin between thumb and forefinger. 'Rather cute.'

He watched her feel the satin, how the soft material slid between her fingers, and counted to ten. Slowly.

It didn't work.

He snagged her fingers and hauled her towards him, their bodies slamming into one another with enough force to leave them winded.

He didn't give her a chance to catch her breath, ravishing

her mouth with the desperation of a man who'd been pushed to his limits.

This idea of his to keep his distance, to keep distractions to a minimum—*so* not working.

Her hands tangled in his hair, finding purchase, as he shoved her against the nearest wall and pressed into her.

She groaned and he deepened the kiss, yearning to be inside her with a hunger that left him reeling.

How could he be this out of control over a woman? One who could never be more than a fling, considering his long-term plans?

Crazy.

The percolator made a god-awful noise as it clicked off, the sound penetrating the sensual cocoon enveloping them.

Sapphire broke the kiss, her chest heaving, her eyes flashing. 'One sugar or two?'

He laughed, easing the tension between them. 'Two. With a double shot of brandy if you have it.'

'Sorry, you'll have to make do with sugar,' she said, busying herself with organising the coffee but unable to hide the betraying tremble in her hands.

He knew the feeling—this relentless, all-consuming craving that had him off-kilter.

Maybe he was going about this all wrong? If an enforced absence wasn't working, maybe he should try the opposite? Getting her out of his system?

It couldn't be any worse than the agonising torture he was going through now.

'Come away with me for the weekend.'

Her hand stilled, holding the kettle in mid-air as she poured boiling water into her mug.

'I thought we were going to not see each other during the campaign—'

'Screw it.' He dragged his hand through his hair and took two steps, which constituted pacing in the tiny kitchenette.

'We need to get this thing out of our systems, and staying apart isn't helping, so let's go for it.'

'Well, when you put it like that, how can a girl refuse?' She topped off her mug and placed the kettle on its stand.

He winced. 'Sorry, that didn't come out right.'

'I get it.' She handed him his coffee. 'We're going a little stir crazy. I guess a weekend away can't hurt.'

'Great. I'll set it up—e-mail you the details.'

She nodded, cradling her mug, staring at him with wide eyes over the top of it.

He couldn't read the expression in those rich blue depths, but if she was half as shell-shocked as him he couldn't blame her.

Hopefully this impulsive weekend away would ease this clamouring attraction between them once and for all. And then he could concentrate on more important things—like putting his plans into action.

'What's got you in a tizz?' Ruby held out an arm, effectively blocking Sapphie's exit from her workshop.

'Nothing,' she said, wishing she hadn't snapped at her sister. It was a sure-fire sign something was going on, considering she'd been nothing but the epitome of calm since Tenang.

Before Patrick showed up, that was.

Ruby pointed to a spare stool next to her workbench. 'Sit. Spill.'

Sapphie shrugged, pretending she didn't have a care in the world, when all she could think about was getting naked with Patrick face to face. Or other bits to other bits, more precisely.

'I'm getting angsty about the show.'

Ruby frowned. 'I thought you weren't allowed to get angsty? Part of your new relaxation routine?'

'There's only so far yoga can take you, Rubes.'

Her sister's astute gaze swept over her. 'This isn't about work, is it?'

''Course it is—'

'Why don't you just bonk him and get it out of your system, already? You'll feel a lot better for it. Trust me.'

Sapphie screwed up her nose. '*Euw!* Please don't elaborate on how you and Jax managed to brainstorm that auction.'

Her sister's smug grin reeked of sin. *Half her luck.*

Ruby laid down her pliers, pushed her loupe out of the way and crossed her arms.

'You've been working like a maniac this last week. Why don't you take the weekend off? Call Patrick? Get together—'

'He's taking me away for the weekend,' she blurted, unable to keep it a secret any longer.

She'd had no intention of telling Ruby anything, expecting to be teased, interrogated or both for the next millennium, but with her departure to destination unknown creeping ever closer Sapphie had to say something for no other reason than articulating made it real.

Ruby clapped. 'Way to go, Saph.' She wiggled her eyebrows. 'Dirty weekend away, huh?'

Sapphie's first instinct was to say *It's not like that*, but after withholding the promise she'd made to their mum on her deathbed and the resultant fallout she'd vowed never to keep the truth from her sister again.

Which meant full disclosure. Within reason.

'I haven't been out with anyone in a while, he seems keen, so it's a bit of harmless fun.'

'Uh-huh.' Ruby nodded, her sly grin particularly worrying. 'So it's just a fling, right? Nothing serious?'

'Yeah.'

'Then why are you so flustered?'

'I'm not,' Sapphie said, making a mockery of her declaration by edging backwards and tripping over a crate.

Ruby chuckled. 'I've never seen you this worked up over a guy before. It's cute.'

'Cute is puppies and newborns. Cute is not the relationship I have with Patrick.'

'Oh? Then what would you call it?'

Raunchy. Decadent. Naughty.

Very, very naughty.

Images of what they'd done in her bathroom and the boardroom and via Skype in her bedroom earlier this week flashed across her memory and heat touched her cheeks.

Ruby held up her hands. 'Never mind. Spare me the details. I can see how good it is written all over your face.' She slugged her on the arm. 'Proud of you.'

At least that made one of them. Sapphie wasn't entirely proud of using Patrick—for that was exactly what she was doing. He wasn't her type, and she had no intention of continuing this dalliance once their work together on Fashion Week ended, so using him didn't sit well.

The fact he seemed more than happy to use her back was a moot point.

'Stop thinking so hard. You'll get frown lines.' Ruby swiped a finger between her brows. 'There's nothing to over-analyse here, sis. Mutual gratification. Fling. Whatever you want to call it— just enjoy.'

She fully intended to. As for what happened after? She'd cross that mannequin when she came to it.

'Where are you taking her?' Serge propped himself on the end of Patrick's desk, the epitome of male chic in one of Fourde's five-grand-a-pop suits.

'What's it to you?' Patrick practically snarled, and instantly regretted it. It wasn't Serge's fault a week's worth of cold showers and iceberg documentaries hadn't taken the edge off. Throw in the lack of sleep from working all hours to distract himself, and he was a grouch.

'Come on, mate, we've always discussed our women in the past.'

He'd deliberately shut the door on his past. And Sapphire was no ordinary woman.

He didn't want to discuss her with Serge, didn't want to hear the usual ribald jokes and innuendo. Sapphire deserved better than that, and the last thing he needed as Fashion Week crept closer was to lose his right-hand man because he'd punched him in the mouth.

Which led to the question: why did he feel so strongly about this? About *her*? He had a job to do in Melbourne: make Australia and the world sit up and take notice of Fourde Fashion's latest branch before he moved on to bigger and better things. That was his primary goal.

Sapphire was great as a temporary distraction but that was all she could ever be. Temporary.

For he had monumental dreams. Ones that involved taking on his folks head-on back in Europe.

Yeah, he'd do well to keep the endgame in sight. Despite the extremely attractive distraction.

Serge slid off his desk and stalked towards a side table, pointing at the basketball-size globe. 'Let me see.' He spun the globe with a finger, jabbing at it to stop it when the map of Australia came around. 'Well, look-ee here.'

Patrick didn't like where this was going. He'd played Serge's stupid flag game in the past, when bedding women had gone in conjunction with partying. Not that he'd ever kept tally of the nationalities of the women he'd slept with, so he could stab a pin into a country as some kind of warped bedpost-notch equivalent, but he'd laughed when Serge had presented him with his round-the-world dalliances.

Later, he'd kept the globe as proof of the life he'd left behind—a life deliberately shunned because it had left him feeling shallow and worthless. Two feelings he'd had a gutful of after his major screw-up.

It served as a visual reminder of how far he'd come and a place he'd never return.

Serge let out a low wolf-whistle. 'Just as I suspected. No flag on Melbourne.'

He hated Serge's sly smirk.

'I'm guessing that's about to change come Monday.'

'I haven't got time for childish games.' Patrick lowered his voice with effort. 'And neither do you. Showtime in two weeks and we're nowhere near ready.'

'Chillax. We'll get there. We always do.'

Patrick wished he had half Serge's confidence. He might be taking charge with Sapphire when it came to sex, but no amount of planning or executing could guarantee a faultless show.

So many variables could go wrong—from a broken stiletto to a thread unravelling, from a model's hissy fit to a competitor sabotaging.

Patrick didn't like the unknown. He intended on planning for every contingency and if that meant working night and day for the next fortnight so be it. After this weekend, that was.

This weekend was all his. And maybe, just maybe, sex with Sapphire would ease his stress levels and make concentrating on work easier.

'If I can't talk about your dirty weekend, can I ask if you've had any feedback from Hardy and Joyce on the Fashion Week presentation?'

Yeah, Patrick had heard from his folks. A vague, general go-ahead while they focussed on more important matters, like booking the Louvre for an innovative Fourde Fashion show or gearing up for Milan.

As if they'd deem the Aussie office worthy of more than a cursory glance.

Well, he had news for them. He'd make them sit up and take notice of Fourde in Melbourne. Then he'd confront them with his plans to take them on in Europe.

They'd probably ignore him again, as they had the first

time he'd mentioned it. When they realised he was for real they wouldn't like it. Worse, they'd probably laugh at him.

But he was sick of being patronised. It seemed nothing he did could make up for the mistakes of the past but this time he intended on making his mark. He'd make them—and the world—pay attention to Patrick Fourde for all the right reasons.

'I don't need their approval,' he said, unclenching his fists beneath the desk.

'Man, you better get laid this weekend because you're wound tight.' Serge shook his head. 'I asked if you'd had feedback, not their approval.'

Sadly, Patrick had a feeling even sex with Sapphire wouldn't alleviate his long-standing stress levels when it came to his folks.

'They're busy as usual. We'll gain their attention soon enough.'

Serge nodded. 'The old Hollywood glamour concept is brilliant. And the designs...' He kissed his fingertips in a flamboyant European gesture. *'Magnifique.'*

Patrick had no doubt his idea would wow the fashion world. What he doubted was gaining the recognition from the two people who mattered the most.

'So you'll be ready for a preview showing first thing Monday morning?'

'Yeah, we'll be ready.' Serge smirked and spun the globe with his finger, hovering over Melbourne again. 'The question is, will you?'

'I'll be here.' He stood, glanced at his watch, making a grand show of having somewhere else to be when in fact he needed to get rid of Serge so he could get on with his plans. 'I've never mixed business with pleasure before and you know it.'

'There's always a first time for everything,' Serge said,

giving the globe a final spin before lumbering towards the door. 'And come Monday there'll be a pin there to prove it.'

Patrick frowned, not liking Serge's immature ribbing, and liking the fact he was probably already mixing business with pleasure less.

CHAPTER SEVEN

'THERE ARE RULES for the weekend.'

Sapphie wriggled in the soft leather seat as Patrick slowed his Ferrari to enter the Southbank precinct. She didn't care what his rules were, as long as they involved the two of them naked. 'Such as?'

'No work talk. No checking e-mails. No leaving the hotel room.'

'But what if I get hungry?'

'You'll get plenty to eat.' He stopped at a red traffic light and shot her a loaded glance packed with sizzle that implied food wouldn't be the only thing on the menu.

Her body pinged in anticipation. 'Any other hoops you want me to jump through?'

'No, but there will be acrobatics involved.'

She laughed at his exaggerated wink as the lights changed and he concentrated on steering through the heavy Friday night traffic.

Banter was good. Banter kept her nerves at bay. And it detracted from the constant doubts whirring through her head as she overanalysed this situation from every angle.

She wanted him. There was no question. But the aftermath? A thousand scenarios, none of them pleasant, plagued her.

Despite his reassurances to keep business and pleasure separate, what if sex screwed things up—literally?

They were both mature, consenting adults with a major attraction going on, but deep down she couldn't quite subdue the tiny voice that kept chanting, *This is Patrick you're going to sleep with.*

The same Patrick who'd tracked down her favourite cola flavoured lollipops when they'd crammed for an exam one week during the school holidays.

The same Patrick who'd collated her assignments and e-mailed the lot when she'd missed a few days with the flu.

The same Patrick who'd rescued her on the night of the grad dance and proved with one scintillating, unforgettable kiss that he wasn't solely the annoying rebel she'd branded him.

And that was what scared her the most. That on some intrinsic level she still craved this guy like a wistful teenager. If those old yearnings were resurrected...

Nope. This was physical all the way. Come Monday they'd revert to work, with a side-serve of flirting.

'We're here.'

Sapphie had been so busy battling with her doubts she'd lost concentration and missed the moment when he steered his boy-toy through the driveway of the Langham Hotel and cut the engine.

'Ready?' His hand sneaked across the console and found hers, his gentle squeeze reassuring.

'Hell, yeah,' she said, earning a wicked grin that made her belly go into freefall.

The next five minutes passed in a blur of bags and valet parking and checking in as Patrick took charge. She liked that about him—how the laid-back guy he'd once been had developed into a go-getter who hadn't lost his ability to have fun.

Decadent weekends away in posh hotels reeked of fun and something she'd never done. She'd stayed in luxurious hotels for work, but never checked in to one with the intention of wallowing in the room.

The new her approved. Spending the weekend holed away was on par with a few hours' meditation or yoga or Pilates.

The old her? Too scared to put in an appearance for fear a stray incense stick would clobber her.

As Patrick handed over his credit card—he'd bristled when she'd insisted on paying half, so she'd let it go for the sake of his manly pride—she glanced around at the exquisite swirled cream marble floors, the sweeping staircase, the fountain cascading water to the ground floor, the stunning floral arrangements.

Combined with the hint of ginger and lemongrass in the air, the Langham exuded a quiet elegance that appealed to her battered soul.

Maybe if she'd taken time out to appreciate places like this over the years she wouldn't have ended up almost losing Seaborns and driving a wedge between her and Ruby in the process?

She'd devoted her life to the company—so many hours she could never take back. At the time she hadn't wanted to, had been content to bury herself in work, but her enforced absence had readjusted her priorities.

When Patrick headed back to Europe she'd make time to do stuff like this, even if it meant checking into a swank hotel for a weekend on her own.

A few spa treatments, a stack of chick-lit novels on her e-reader and Room Service would be the perfect antidote to her frenetic schedule.

And if she'd probably remember this time with one of the sexiest guys she'd ever met and maybe crave him a tad? She'd better make sure they created some pretty unforgettable memories this weekend to resurrect when needed.

'Let's go.'

His breath fanned her ear as he placed a hand in the small of her back. The simple touch sent a shiver of longing through her.

He must have felt the faintest tremor, for his fingers

strummed her spine on the way to her neck, where he caressed the exposed skin. 'The faster we hit room 2227, the faster we get to unpack those boxes.'

She almost corrected him and said suitcases—until she realised what he meant. While her body couldn't wait to hit that room, her rationale couldn't be ignored completely.

Her hands cupped his face, leaving him no option but to look into her eyes. 'We're really doing this? I mean, we still have to work together, and what if—?'

He kissed her—a soft, tender sweep across her lips that had her melting into him.

'I picked a hotel because I wanted this to be special. Not a quickie in your apartment or on my desk.' He raised an eyebrow. 'Though that's not entirely out of the question later.'

Okay, so he wanted a 'later'? Before she could ponder or question what that meant, he continued.

'We've known each other a long time so there's no pretences, no awkwardness later. We indulge ourselves, have a memorable weekend without regrets.' His arms slid around her waist, anchoring her. 'You with me?'

With her heart still questioning the validity of what she was about to do, she nodded. 'All the way.'

All the way echoed through her head as the elevator whisked them to the twenty-second floor and their exclusive Club suite.

It continued to plague her as he deftly swiped the key card and held open the door for her.

Then she stepped into the room and her fears faded.

Sapphie had a keen eye for beauty. It came with the territory of being groomed by a society mother who'd prided herself on appearance and showing the world grace and elegance at all costs. Growing up surrounded by exquisite jewels, being the spokesperson for Seaborns, had developed that keen eye. So stepping into the gorgeous Club room should have sent her observatory radar onto high alert.

Instead, the floral embossed carpet, the deep green drapes, the luxurious Old Worlde furnishings and the amazing view of Melbourne's Flinders St Station, Federation Square and surrounds faded into oblivion the moment Patrick closed the door and backed her up against the nearest wall.

'I've been going frigging nuts with wanting you,' he said, kissing her before she could respond.

That tender kiss in the lobby had been nothing like this. Desperation. Hunger. Insanity. All combined to make her press against him as if she'd never get enough.

Sex in the past had been okay. Probably more her fault than the guys she'd dated, because her mind would always wander to business and she'd be mentally making lists instead of making whoopee.

But Patrick's passionate kiss and the way his hands were tearing at her clothes… Her mind delightfully blanked.

She ripped at his shirt. Buttons flew.

He tugged at her skirt. The zip stuck.

They swore in unison, laughed, and their fingers became more dextrous as pants, tops and underwear were stripped in haste and protection donned.

'Finally,' he said, his gaze hot and potent as he started at her chest and swept downwards. 'You're as beautiful as I imagined.'

Sapphie's first instinct was to squirm, but she forced herself to stand still beneath his scrutiny. People had stared at her over the years when she'd been modelling Seaborns' jewels but that was different.

No one had ever made her feel so thoroughly exposed as Patrick did at that moment.

'You have no idea how long I've been fantasising about this.' He reached out, tracing a nipple with his fingertip. 'And it's way better in reality.'

'Good to hear,' she breathed on a sigh as he stepped closer, his erection brushing her abdomen. 'Because I haven't been thinking about you at all.'

He laughed and pressed harder against her. 'Well, then, I'll have to change all that.'

His hands cupped her butt, hoisted her up, and she instinctively wrapped her legs around him. 'What I plan on doing to you this weekend will be unforgettable.'

Sapphie didn't doubt it. That was the plan anyway: store up amazing memories for the long nights ahead when she mulled over how to make Seaborns bigger and better.

The Fashion Week campaign might keep the company in the black for years to come but she'd never stop striving. It had been her mum's dream, was too ingrained, and while she intended on taking more time out in the future it didn't mean she'd ever stop taking Seaborns to the top.

'You're that confident?'

'Want me to prove it to you?'

He nuzzled her neck and she moaned. 'Please do.'

He eased back a tad and tried to slide a hand between their bodies but she stopped him.

'You've pleasured me enough. This time's all about you.'

His eyes darkened to slate as he remembered the times in the bathroom, the boardroom.

'I want you inside me. Now.'

'I like it when you're bossy,' he said, sliding into her with one long thrust. 'A woman who knows what she wants is such a turn-on.'

He eased out and she could have sworn she whimpered— a needy sound so out of character her she froze in surprise.

'In that case, I want you to…' She whispered exactly how hard and fast she wanted him in his ear, her cheeks burning the entire time.

But knowing how much Patrick wanted her, feeling him fill her, was incredibly empowering.

When her last command faded on a whisper Patrick took over. Hoisting her higher. Driving into her harder. Gripping her tighter as every thrust drove her closer to release.

She'd never achieved release by internal stimulation alone, but as Patrick talked dirty and demonstrated how he could follow through the tension in her muscles built and coiled in a delicious combination of pleasure bordering on pain.

'Patrick, jeez...' She shattered, spasms making her shudder a moment before he joined her on a drawn out groan.

They didn't move for several long seconds as Sapphie tried to comprehend the enormity of what had just happened.

She'd just had her first cataclysmic, fabled internal climax. And while it had been monumentally stupendous, with her body still trembling in aftershocks, she couldn't ignore the niggle of concern—the one that insisted the connection she'd just experienced with Patrick was one in a million.

Closely followed by a thought: what the hell would she do when he left?

Patrick's grand plans to keep Sapphire locked away in their hotel room for the entire weekend hit a hurdle on Saturday.

He had to get out.

If he didn't he was in dire danger of doing something he'd sworn he'd never do.

Committing to a woman.

The sex was phenomenal, but it was more than that. It was the shared laughter and confidences in bed last night, the common cravings for buttered popcorn and orange soda while watching an action flick, the crazy, scary feeling of total 'rightness' being with her induced.

He'd dated a lot of women the world over, but not one had managed to get under his skin as quickly as Sapphire.

How had the prissy, uptight kid from school turned into this temptress?

He'd expected his raging hunger for her to abate after last

night. It hadn't. If anything he had serious concerns he'd never be able to get her out of his head again.

Not good, considering their goals were worlds apart.

She had a high-end Melbourne jewellery institution to run, he had grand plans to take on his folks head-on in Europe.

Yep, worlds apart.

Where did that leave him? He'd gone into this with few expectations: short-term fling, move on.

So why, after spending one incredible night in her arms, had that thought become unpalatable?

'Good to know you're a rule-breaker.' Sapphire raised her G&T in his direction. 'Mighty generous of you, letting me leave the room.'

He gestured around the exclusive Club lounge on the twenty-fourth floor. 'Didn't want to push my luck with you getting bored of me. Thought you might appreciate a change of scenery.'

'No chance of that.' She sipped at her drink. It did little to cool the telltale blush staining her cheeks. 'For much as I love the incredible city views and drinks and amazing scared scallops, I think you have plenty to offer by way of entertainment.'

He grinned as her blush deepened. 'You think I'm entertaining, huh?' He beckoned her closer and murmured in her ear. 'Would that be when I'm going down on you or taking you from behind in the shower?'

'Shh,' she said, and shoved him away—but not before he'd glimpsed the hint of a smug smile. The smile of a satisfied, multiple-pleasured woman who hadn't been reticent about letting him know.

Another thing that had surprised him—her absolute joyful abandonment when it came to sex. Sure, she'd been responsive in her bathroom and his boardroom, but he hadn't expected her to be so utterly horny.

There was something infinitely appealing about a woman

who enjoyed sex and wasn't afraid to show it, and he loved that beneath her cool, businesswoman façade she was a sexpot vixen.

And she was all his.

At least for the weekend.

'You're really enjoying this, aren't you?'

Her eyes lit up with pleasure and she nodded. 'Not dismissing the last twenty-four hours in our suite, I'm having a ball being here.' She beckoned him closer with a crook of her finger. 'I never do stuff like this. Feels like I'm playing hooky and I love it.'

'Don't you go away for girls' weekends with Ruby?'

Shadows blanketed the light in her eyes and the corners of her mouth drooped. 'We've been pretty busy keeping Seaborns afloat since Mum died, so most of our weekends have been spent working.'

Her response surprised him. Sure, he'd heard the rumours about Seaborns being in financial trouble but that had only been recently. As far as he knew the jeweller was a Melbourne institution and supplied pieces to the stars.

It looked as if a lot had happened in his absence.

'I thought Mathilda was an astute businesswoman?'

Sapphire gnawed on her bottom lip, her G&T forgotten. 'She was, but the shoddy economy hit us hard. Even rich folk stopped spending big on frivolities like new bracelets or necklaces and our profit margins tightened.' She shook her head. 'I made a promise to Mum to do whatever it took to keep Seaborns lucrative.'

'You're doing a great job—'

'I almost lost the company,' she said, her tone soft and plaintive. 'Pushed myself too hard, didn't enlist Ruby's help—would've collapsed with a healthy dose of chronic fatigue syndrome if I hadn't taken an enforced leave of absence.'

'I didn't know.'

'Not many people do. Rubes did a great job keeping us viable while I recuperated at a health spa near Daylesford.'

'How long?'

'Three months.'

He couldn't imagine this successful, driven woman taking a week off, let alone twelve weeks, and that fact rammed home how bad it must've been.

'How do you feel now?'

'Invigorated.' She raised her glass in his direction, her smile self-deprecating. 'Thanks to you.'

She'd given him an opportunity to dismiss the heavy stuff she'd revealed and move onto familiar teasing territory.

He wanted to—didn't want to delve into personal territory that might strengthen the bonds between them. But the shadows in her eyes remained and he'd be damned if he'd let her down now she'd opened up. He might not want to complicate what they shared by taking it further, but the least he could do was hear her out if she wanted to offload.

'When did you return to work?'

A slight frown creased her forehead. 'The week before you walked in on me.'

He swore. 'So you take months off and then jump straight back into the fray by pitching for the Fourde show?'

She glared at him, sass and defiance, and he'd never wanted to hold a woman more than he did at that moment.

'I'd done my time. Rested, chilled, unburdened my soul to a bunch of self-help groups. Meditated, stretched—you name it, I probably tried it. But in the end...' She made a circular motion with her finger at her temple. 'I was going a little stir-crazy with all that wholesome goodness.'

'Understandable. But we've been working manic hours on this show. How are you holding up?'

'You tell me.' She actually winked, obliterating the seriousness of their conversation. 'At the risk of your ego getting any bigger than it already is, hanging out with you has been good for me.'

'Care to clarify "hanging out"?'

'At work.' Her coy glance from beneath lowered lashes was adorable. 'Out of work.'

'In clothes.' He ran a fingertip down her bare forearm, savoured her involuntary reaction as he raised goosebumps. 'Out of clothes.'

She smiled, the tension of the last few minutes gone.

'If I'd known you'd be better for me than months' worth of yoga and meditation I'd have considered flying to Europe.'

She'd meant it as a light-hearted quip, a continuation of their word-play. But hot on the heels of his realisation that their fragile relationship could never go further it stung.

In a hypothetical world, if she were free from responsibilities, would they have a future?

Fruitless, irrelevant musings. But for a moment, with the thought of her joining him in Europe, it had been nice to dream.

He raised his Scotch and clinked it against her glass. 'Well, lucky you don't have to travel to Europe for my exclusive services. You can have as much as you want of me right here.'

'I'll drink to that.'

She took a sip, lowered her glass and pinned him with a curious stare. 'What's it like working in Paris? Must be ultra glam.'

Unease tightened his throat. He didn't want to talk about his life in Paris. Didn't want to run the risk of saying stuff he shouldn't. But she'd opened up to him with surprising honesty. The least he could do was give her a snippet.

'It's competitive. All the best fashion houses in the world vie for attention there.'

'Yet Fourde Fashion continues to thrive? Your folks must be proud.'

Her steady stare never wavered, and along with the lies

he'd now have to tell came the wish he'd changed the subject when he'd had the chance.

'The business is their baby. As long as Fourde flourishes all is right with the world.'

He tried to keep the bitterness out of his voice but Sapphire was smart, and by the slight frown crinkling her brows he knew she must have picked up on the hint of hostility in his tone.

'Can be tough, working for your folks.' She swirled her drink absentmindedly, took a sip. 'I adored Mum but she was a ruthless boss. And being family muddied the boundaries sometimes.'

If she only knew. His familial boundaries weren't muddied—they were clearly obliterated.

'Yeah, can make for interesting employee evaluations.'

Not that he'd been subjected to any from his folks. They preferred to let their silent disapproval do the talking.

'I used to envy you.' She snuggled into her seat and cupped her hands around her glass. 'Not having parents looking over your shoulder all the time.'

'They would've had to care to do that,' he blurted, instantly regretting his blunt response when her eyes widened in surprise.

'You didn't get along?'

He shrugged, wishing he'd kept his big mouth shut, trying to play down his obvious resentment after that clanger.

'I was a late arrival—a mid-life mistake. They had a burgeoning business and self-sufficient teenagers when I arrived. The rest is self-explanatory.'

Her pity was palpable. 'So you didn't spend much time together as a family?'

'Try none.' This time he managed to keep the acrimony out of his voice. 'But, hey, as you said, I got to spend my last years of school parent-free. Lucky me.'

Then why did he feel so unlucky?

'Bet they're glad you're all making up for lost time now.'

He grunted in response. Enough with discussing families, already. 'Another drink?'

Thankfully she let him change the subject.

'I haven't finished this one yet.' She glanced at the half-empty glass in her hand and raised an eyebrow. 'Are you trying to get me drunk so you can take advantage of me?'

He winked. 'Newsflash, sweetheart. I don't need you tipsy to do that.'

'Good point.' Her eyes darkened to midnight as the tip of her tongue swept along her bottom lip, eliciting an instant tightening in the vicinity of his groin.

'I need a refill,' he said, also needing to get this evening back onto light-hearted ground. 'Maybe you can take advantage of me?'

She laughed. 'Keep wishing.'

As they continued their banter while feasting on delicious dips and breads, flirting outrageously, Patrick couldn't dismiss the niggling feeling he'd be missing out on something great when he followed his dream in Europe.

And for the first time ever he wondered if it was worth it.

CHAPTER EIGHT

SAPPHIE WASN'T IMAGINING the deep freeze.

Patrick had been distracted during breakfast this morning, cool at check-out, and more distant the closer they got to Armidale.

When he parked outside Seaborns she could have created ice carvings—the chill in the car was that palpable.

She knew what he was doing. Deliberately establishing distance between them after the intimacy of the weekend. Understandable, considering the manic fortnight ahead of them before Fashion Week. She'd pretty much planned on doing the same thing—withdrawing on a subtle level to concentrate on work.

What she hadn't planned on was feeling this…this…*bereft*. As if she'd had something wonderful, lost it, and was now grieving.

Crazy, as she'd known what this was going in: a short-term fling and some much needed fun after a disastrous twelve months. A rotten two years, in fact.

Since her mum had died, when was the last time she'd had fun? Had a weekend off for that matter?

She hadn't, and it made the last forty-eight hours all the more precious. Physically, she'd wanted to prove something to herself, and the weekend with Patrick had done that and more.

Withdrawing was one thing, but feeling this crappy because of it was not good.

She hadn't expected to feel like this—didn't want to feel like this for the next two weeks—so she had no option but to draw attention to the obvious: iciness didn't foster good working relations.

'You're coming in to check out the latest designs?'

Patrick glanced at his watch, reluctance radiating off him. 'Yeah, but just for a few minutes. I'm heading to the office for the afternoon.'

'I thought I was the only workaholic who'd forgo a gorgeous Sunday arvo for the office?'

He shrugged. 'It's how success is bred.'

'Wow,' she said, wishing he'd smile or wink or give some semblance of the laid-back charmer she loved. *Liked.* 'This from the guy who had to be bribed to show up for study weekends?'

Finally a flicker of light in his eyes. 'Those Dairy Bell milkshakes were so worth it.'

'Not my scintillating company?'

He snorted. 'You were an acid-tongued killjoy when it came to hitting the books.'

'How do you think you're successful now?'

'Good looks and charm?'

She rolled her eyes, secretly thrilled he was thawing. 'Throw in modesty.'

At last the corners of his mouth eased into the lazy grin that never failed to make her heart skip a beat.

'Did you ever think we'd end up here?'

She had no idea if he meant professionally or personally.

He gestured towards Seaborns' shopfront. 'I guess you always knew you'd be running this one day. It's all you ever focussed on—getting good grades, working here part-time.' He blew out a long breath, his expression pensive. 'Me? I didn't have a clue.'

Interestingly, they hadn't discussed how he'd ended up working in fashion. She'd assumed he'd entered the family business like her, by living up to familial expectations. But, considering his revelations regarding his folks over the weekend, she found it surprising he'd choose to work with them. It sounded as if they'd been rotten parents and he still bore the emotional scars, so how had he ended up fronting their fashion house in Australia?

'You had grand plans to travel during a gap year. What made you enter fashion?'

What little headway she'd made in re-establishing warmth vanished as the shutters descended, effectively wiping the warmth from his eyes.

'I fell into it,' he said, staring out through the windscreen at nothing in particular. 'Did an internship, studied part-time, then needed time away. Got bored with travelling after a while. Had a Marketing degree under my belt. Dropped by the Paris office more regularly on my return.'

There was more to it—a lot more, judging by the rigid shoulders and compressed lips—but now wasn't the time to push.

'Well, I for one am glad you did, because together with Seaborns you're going to take Fashion Week by storm.'

'Hope so,' he muttered, tearing his gaze away from a tram trundling by to turn towards her. 'You know how busy we're going to be the next few weeks, right?'

Ah, here it comes. The brush-off.

She could make it easy for him, but what they'd shared wasn't two strangers hooking up for a dirty weekend and then going their separate ways.

They shared a past—albeit a platonic high school friendship. And they shared a professional bond that would single-handedly take Seaborns into a new stratosphere.

She—they—deserved more.

'Agreed,' she said. 'I'm assuming a busy work schedule precludes us from having sex?'

Her bluntness surprised him. An eyebrow twitched.

'I'm trying to make this easier on both of us—'

'Don't.' She shook her head. 'Don't give me some lame spiel you've probably used on a million women before.'

This time his jaw dropped a tad.

'We're both professionals, with a clear goal in sight, and we're going to get there. But if what's happened over the last few weeks is any indication, that spark we share can't be turned off because we've pulled an all-nighter or have spreadsheets to prepare. So let's not waste time doing this.'

She waved a hand between the two of them. 'You and me? Phenomenal sex. So why don't we see how it goes over the next few weeks? If we have a spare moment and our schedules coincide we hook up.'

'You're something else,' he said, staring at her with undisguised admiration. 'And for the record? Thousands of women, not millions.'

She punched him on the arm.

'And the reason why I've cooled off today is because spending the weekend with you has solidified what I already knew.' His hand snaked across, captured hers. 'The reality of being with you far surpassed the fantasy and it's doing my head in.'

Okay, she hadn't expected that.

'I really like you, but I don't have room in my life right now for complications.'

'Jeez, thanks. Way to go with the flattery.'

His sheepish smile made her want to hug him. 'I need to make this show work before…'

He squeezed her hand, released it, his look away not inspiring her with confidence.

'Before…?' she prompted, her rampant curiosity filling in the blanks.

Before he absconded to the Pacific with a Bond girl?

Before he revealed his secret harem?

Or, the most likely, before he headed back to Paris?

'Everything's up in the air at the moment, so I can't really talk about it.' He swiped a hand over his face. It did little to ease the tension lines bracketing his mouth. 'I don't want to lead you on or build false hopes. I can't be any clearer than that.'

'So what was the weekend about?'

'Selfishness.' He drummed his fingers against the steering wheel, as if he couldn't wait to escape. 'Ever want something so badly when you finally get it you can't quite believe it's real?'

Yeah, that was how she'd initially felt about assuming control of Seaborns. Until she'd realised she was more enamoured of the idea of being in charge than the reality. Her mum had built up the place, had constructed her dreams around it, and she'd happily gone along with it.

But poring over sales figures at midnight and haggling with diamond mines over undercutting prices wasn't quite as glamorous as she'd been led to believe, and while walking through the showroom still gave her a buzz it wasn't quite the same buzz being with Patrick over the weekend had given her.

'I want you even more now, if that's possible, but I won't jerk you around.' He eyeballed her. 'I may be gone in three weeks and I don't want you hurt.'

Having him articulate the inevitable should have allayed her fears and reinforced her decision to view this as purely a fling. So why did his last words echo through her head like a mournful warning?

A warning she should heed if she knew what was good for her. But that was just the point. Patrick was good for her. She'd felt more alive, more buzzed over the weekend than she had in years.

She liked the feeling. Liked the uncharacteristic feeling of invincibility it gave her. For someone who'd been on the brink of not being able to get out of bed because her muscles wouldn't co-operate, it was a heady high and a power-ful aphrodisiac.

She wanted more.

Even if her potent medicine had an end-date stamped all over it.

'We can squeeze a lot of fun into three weeks,' she said, proud her voice didn't give a hint of her inner turmoil.

She wanted him.

She didn't want him to leave.

She didn't want to get too attached.

It was a confusing jumble, making her want to shake him or kiss him. She hadn't decided which yet.

'How can a guy say no to that?'

'You can't.'

She opened the car door, grabbed her bag and headed for Seaborns with Patrick not far behind.

He'd finally fallen in with her plans but he might need a little convincing.

And she knew just the way to do it.

Patrick checked out the dazzling display of jewellery Ruby had created for Fashion Week, snagged a yellow diamond choker on his finger and held it out to Sapphire.

'Model it for me.'

'Sure,' she said, reaching for it.

He raised his arm, waved the necklace just out of reach. 'Naked.'

She elbowed him. 'If you want to see me wear it—fine. But the clothes stay on.' In a slick move involving an armpit tickle and a semi-jump, she recovered the choker. 'For now.'

'I'll hold you to that,' he said, meaning it. He'd hold her all night long if he had his way, but he had to leave. If he didn't get out of here soon who knew what he'd divulge?

He'd been close to blurting the truth—all of it—in the car.

She'd been so open, not pulling any punches like most

women he knew. Guileless and honest, stating what she wanted in clear terms. No room for misunderstandings. No unrealistic expectations.

She knew he'd be leaving.

And it didn't matter.

He should be high-fiving.

A short-term sexual dalliance without complications.

Instead it had made him think. Why didn't she want more? They were good together. She'd admitted it. So why didn't she want to consider continuing this relationship beyond a month?

Not that he wanted to do long distance, or anything remotely like it, but to have her dismiss anything beyond a fling as a possibility kinda stung. Stupid guy pride.

He'd thought he'd stuffed up, revealing all that stuff about his folks and their neglect. Emotional baggage usually had women wanting to delve and analyse and grow closer.

Not Sapphire. She'd done the opposite—proposing they continue with the sex with an end-date in sight.

He couldn't fathom it.

The gentlemanly thing to do would be not to take advantage of the situation. To say, *Thanks, Saph, I've had a great time but sleeping together will ensure we grow closer over the next few weeks and neither one of us wants that...* Ah, hell. Maybe the gentleman in him should shut up.

This was why he didn't do relationships. They confused the hell out of him.

He'd deliberately pushed her away, terrified of the closeness they'd established over the weekend. He'd never told any woman about his folks—least of all a woman he had feelings for.

Feelings?

Uh-uh. No way. He needed to amend that to a woman he was *at risk of developing feelings for*. Yeah, much better.

Jeez, he could be an idiot. All the amendments in the world wouldn't change facts: he might have agreed to take advantage of Sapphire's offer and continue the sex for as long as he was around, but pretending he didn't feel more for her would be tough.

He should have stuck to his guns and ended it in the car as he'd intended. It would have been easier than this floundering, out-of-control feeling that made him contemplate crazy things—*long distance things*—he had no intention of following up on.

'Sure you don't want to see the pieces with the gowns?'

Her voice drifted out from the bedroom, soft and alluring, and it took every ounce of his limited willpower not to barge in there and say *Screw the jewellery*.

'Designers' meeting is first thing in the morning, so it would be great to get a sneak peek at them now,' he said, managing to sound businesslike when all he could think about was her strutting back into the room wearing a diamond necklace and towering stilettos only. Totally making a mockery of his moral dilemma a few moments ago.

He'd never been a gentleman. No point starting now.

'Okay, you asked for it.'

She strutted into the room wearing a sheer black lace teddy, suspenders, stockings and stilettos. Oh, and the necklace was somewhere in the vicinity of her neck, but he was too busy checking out the rest to notice.

Yep, that inner gentleman was long gone now.

'Are you trying to give me a heart attack?' He clutched at his chest and pretended to stagger.

'Nothing wrong with your heart if that workout over the weekend was any indication.'

She struck a provocative pose, mischief lighting her eyes. 'You've seen this piece. Shall I try on the next?'

'No.'

He strode towards her with one thing on his mind—and it wasn't the carats of diamonds draping her neck.

'But what about the designers' meeting in the morning and needing to see them before then?'

'Screw the meeting,' he muttered, sweeping the small desk behind her clean and pinning her against it. 'I have more important things on my mind.'

She wriggled against his hard-on. 'Like?'

'You. Me. Naked.'

'You're fixated on the naked thing.'

'I'm fixated on you.'

The teddy looked hot, but it was a pain in the ass to undo so he did the only logical thing. Ripped it.

'Caveman,' she said, her smile saucy.

'Wait 'til you see my club.'

She groaned at his pun—or it might have been due to his tongue working its way down to her breast.

He sucked her nipple into his mouth, laved it while easing a finger inside her at the same time.

She was so eager, so responsive, so hot.

'Patrick...'

She grabbed his head and practically dragged him up to meet her mouth, demanding and ravenous.

He loved how she matched him, clamorous and unrelenting, striving for satisfaction.

Her tongue taunted him as he unzipped and sheathed himself in record time.

Her hands grabbed his butt and hauled him closer as he propped her on the desk.

Her body arched and her head fell back as he thrust into her with one stroke.

She gripped the edge of the desk. He gripped her hips.

She watched him drive into her, eyes wide and dazed. He watched her and had never been so turned on in all his life.

She came hard and fast, clenching around him, sighing his name. He came a second later, exploding into her with a force that made his head snap back.

'Thanks for making my desk fantasy come true,' she said, flushed and sated and utterly ravishing.

'My pleasure,' he said, when in fact he wanted to thank her for being his fantasy come true.

His hopes to focus solely on work these next few weeks were royally screwed. Like him.

For, come the end of this Fashion Week campaign, he knew he didn't have a hope in hell of walking away from this.

Sapphie ran a face-washer over her skin, aware they had a ton of work to do despite it being Sunday afternoon.

However, the speedy scrub with the small towel didn't invigorate her skin half as much as the sensual encounter with Patrick a few moments ago.

It had been a test.

Ironically, she wasn't sure if she'd passed or failed.

She might have just proved she could physically continue this relationship without any future, but her insistent voice of reason, the one nagging nonstop that she was being foolish, wouldn't shut up.

The smart thing to have done when he'd given her the brush off earlier in the car would have been to end this *thing* between them. They'd had a great time, worked the attraction out of their systems, and now could focus on work.

Well, from his spiel maybe *he* could, but no way would she be able to work closely with him over the next three weeks and pretend she hadn't seen him naked, hadn't kissed him all over, hadn't touched him, held him…

She scrubbed her face again. It did little for her flaming cheeks.

She could justify her decision to prolong their sexual relationship as the best kind of therapy for her body. She hadn't felt this good in years…blah, blah, blah.

While that might be true—and she revelled in feeling physically empowered for the first time in yonks—she knew continuing their relationship had more to do with the emotional connection they'd reluctantly established over the weekend than anything else.

And she didn't want an emotional connection. Had deliberately seduced him fifteen minutes ago because of it. Determined to prove to herself she could handle the sex and little else.

Instead all she'd proved was what she'd known all along: the sex was incredible. And maybe they could be too, given half a chance.

She flung away the face-washer in disgust, poked her tongue out at her reflection, and shimmied into the nearest clothes handy: a faded rock band T-shirt—one of Ruby's remnants—and a denim skirt.

She didn't have time for a relationship even if she wanted one, and it looked like Patrick felt the same way.

She needed to prove she could be the best leader Seaborns had ever had, and by the sounds of it Patrick had a lot to prove to his folks even if he didn't know it yet.

When he'd opened up about his upbringing it had been pretty obvious where his bitterness sprang from. They'd neglected him as a kid so he'd probably go all out as an adult to show them what he was capable of. Gain the attention he'd never had.

And she hoped he'd succeed. For while Mathilda had been a tough taskmaster, her mum had always been there for her and she couldn't imagine it otherwise.

Yeah, best for her to strive to be the best and for Patrick to chase his dreams. She should be thankful they'd both been perfectly clear in the car. No expectations. No regrets.

So why did her heart give a little lurch as she exited the bathroom and caught sight of him waiting for her?

As Sapphire walked Patrick out a flash of white gold caught his eye.

He'd strolled through this showroom several times now,

was almost immune to the precious gems and stunning creations cradled lovingly on midnight-blue velvet behind glass-enclosed cases highlighted by muted light.

What captured his attention about this piece was where it was situated—tucked into a corner, almost invisible behind the more dazzling displays up front.

'What's wrong?'

'Nothing,' he said, holding onto Sapphire's hand as he detoured towards the cabinet. 'Why's this piece hidden away?'

'Poor seller.' Sapphire shrugged. 'Ruby loves creating modern stuff for fun—has a whole storeroom full of it—but no one wants to buy it.'

As Patrick stared at the lightning bolt white gold and jade pendant edged in pinpoint diamonds a buzz of creative excitement zapped his gut.

This was the kind of piece that would have accessorised his first show perfectly—the kind of edgy, contemporary vibe he loved. But the traditional fashionistas in Europe didn't.

Staring at Ruby's exquisite piece of modern art, he felt a long-suppressed urge stir to life. He had grand plans to instigate when he returned to Paris shortly, but why not give the fashion world a little pre-emptive taste?

'How adventurous are you?'

A faint pink stained Sapphire's cheeks. 'Considering what we just did on the desk upstairs, you tell me.'

He tugged her in for a quick kiss on the lips, determinedly ignoring the urge to deepen it.

'I'm thinking of running a little adjunct to our fashion show. Something edgy. Funky. Contemporary.' He pointed at the lightning bolt. 'Showcasing modern fashion with pieces like that.'

Sapphire gaped. 'But the timeline… It's impossible—'

'You said Ruby has a storeroom full of modern pieces like this?'

'Yeah, but co-ordinating the fashion on top of our current workload…how do you expect to pull this off?'

He wanted to blurt the entire truth, wanted to trust her. But she'd doubted him at the start—doubted he could co-ordinate something as big as the old Hollywood glamour campaign—how would she feel if she knew the extent of his plans for his modern series?

'I've had designers do some mock-ups for a contemporary show I'm planning in Paris. Wouldn't take long for Ruby to have a look, match the jewellery.'

She stared at him with an ego-boosting mix of awe and admiration. 'You're serious about this?'

'Absolutely.' He gently tapped the glass cabinet. 'Wouldn't it be great if Seaborns started selling more of this stuff too?'

'Rubes would love you for ever,' she said, peering closer at the pendant. And it would be so good to give something back to her. 'Given a choice, she'd rather create contemporary stuff like this every day of the week. If she had a chance to show some of it at Fashion Week she'd freak out.'

'Good. That's settled.'

He squeezed her hand and released it. 'I'll get the designs couriered over later and let you get to work co-ordinating the pieces.'

'Okay.' Sapphire stared at him as if she still couldn't quite believe they were doing this. 'Have to say I'm surprised.'

'By?'

'Fourde Fashion's signature couture is all about timeless elegance.' Her quick doubtful glance at Ruby's lightning bolt spoke volumes. 'Isn't this confusing the brand a tad?'

That was putting it mildly. It wouldn't just confuse the Fourde brand, it would give his folks a coronary.

Which was why he had no intention of launching this event under the Fourde Fashion label.

He'd planned on doing it when he returned to Paris shortly. But this could be a perfect opportunity. How this short collection was received would be a fair indication if the European market were ready for him or not.

It hadn't been a decade earlier, but a lot had changed in ten years. *He'd* changed in ten years, and no longer would he be quashed into thinking his ideas were wrong or unsuitable.

His mistake back then had been trying to fit a bright, shiny new idea under the guise of a long-established vintage company.

This time he'd be using his name all the way.

The buck stopped with him.

'I'm thinking of producing this independent of the Fourde label.'

She paused, a tiny frown creasing her brow, and he half expected her to renege. Hitching Seaborns to the successful Fourde Fashion wasn't a problem, but would she be up for the risk associated with an unknown brand?

The astute businesswoman he knew her to be wouldn't go for it. And the fact she'd asked the question signalled her doubts. Doubts in him.

And he hated it. Hated that no matter how far they'd come, both personally and professionally, she didn't deem him capable enough.

'You have a problem with that?'

His tone sounded way too harsh and her frown deepened.

'Actually, I'm thinking it's better this way. Break away from the established mould.' She tapped her lower lip, deep in thought. 'Fashion peeps will have expectations of anything that launches under the Fourde Fashion label, and you don't want something new and innovative to be unfairly judged because it's not the norm.'

Some of his anger faded at her insight. She'd pretty much honed in on the number one reason he'd failed the first time around. And why he wouldn't make the same mistake again.

'Exactly. Modern and edgy isn't what Fourde is renowned for.'

She hadn't lost the frown. 'You're up against your employer. In direct competition with your folks.'

'They know I'm keen to branch out.'

True enough. He'd mentioned it on several occasions—not that they'd given his aspirations much credit.

As long as he kept performing for Fourde they weren't terribly concerned about where he expended his creative energy.

They'd assumed the failure of his first showing would maim his desire to break into contemporary fashion. No great surprise. They didn't know him well, didn't know he used the bitter rejection of that first show as the spur that drove him every day.

'If you say so.'

By the dubious twist to her mouth he hadn't allayed all her doubts. No matter. He'd add her to the list of people he had to prove something to.

'I'll call you,' he said, dropping a kiss on her cheek. 'We'll chat after you've seen the designs later today.'

'No worries,' she said, but as he eased out through the door and glanced over his shoulder that groove slashing her forehead said she had worries indeed.

Irrelevant. Patrick would prove he had something to offer the fashion world.

Today Melbourne. Tomorrow the world.

'Can't believe we pulled this together in five days,' Sapphie said, shaking her head as the last model took to the catwalk, wearing a leopard print mini-jumpsuit and a funky rose-gold topaz necklace and earring combo, to another round of rapturous applause from the audience.

'The Fashion Week organisers were happy to squeeze me in.' Patrick rubbed his thumb and forefinger together. 'Guess the fact Fourde Fashion is sponsoring the main event helped them see the wisdom of supporting the launch of this indie collection.'

'I think the designs have helped sell the collection more.' She laid a hand on his arm, relishing the innocuous touch. Working on this contemporary show had been a blast, but the fact they hadn't had a spare second to play had her jumpy. 'They're seriously good. Cutting edge stuff.'

'Thanks,' he said, not taking his eyes off the model as she did her final pose at the end of the catwalk before strutting back towards them. 'Let's hope the critics agree with you.'

'They will.' She gestured towards the other models, waiting in the wings for the finale when all the designs would be on the catwalk at once. 'Bold colours. Textured fabrics. Short diagonal hems. Asymmetrical necklines. A pretty eye-catching combination.'

'Don't forget the jewellery,' he said, some of the tension in his rigid shoulders easing. 'We're a package deal.'

'And doesn't Ruby know it?' Sapphie jerked a thumb over her shoulder in the direction of her sister, who flitted between the models ensuring clasps were fastened tight and earrings clipped and bracelets snug.

She'd seen Ruby animated backstage before, but the fact her sister had an extra pep in her step was obvious. Ruby had freaked when she'd heard about the chance to showcase her contemporary designs, and had worked two all-nighters to ensure Patrick's outfits were perfectly paired with the right jewellery.

Sapphie had to admit she'd been wary at first of taking a risk with designs not backed by the Fourde Fashion name. But then she'd seen the clothes, and there had been no denying this was a golden opportunity to promote Seaborns in a whole new light.

Moving into a contemporary market would be a dream come true for Ruby, and anything that put a permanent smile on her sis's face was fine by her. Ruby deserved it after all she'd done for her and the company over the last year.

Ruby and Jax had singlehandedly wiped out the mortgage

she'd taken out on the showroom and her place, and had cemented Seaborns as a force to be reckoned with again.

They'd given her a chance to resume leadership duties on her terms and she'd always be grateful. Proving she could physically handle the job would have been ten times harder if she'd had to deal with financial woes too.

She wanted these designs to rock—wanted the public to love Ruby's creative genius as much as she did.

By the rousing applause from the crowd, they were well on their way.

'Let the finale begin,' Patrick muttered as the models took to the catwalk *en masse*.

The noise from the crowd crescendoed amid myriad camera flashes, and the hoots, stomping and wolf whistles were vindication that she'd done the right thing in taking a chance on Patrick.

Which begged the question: How far was she willing to go to really take a chance on him with what mattered? Her heart...

'Can you hear that?' He stared at her in wide-eyed wonder before letting out an exultant whoop and hoisting her high, spinning her around until she was dizzy. 'They love us.'

She laughed as he lowered her back to her feet. 'Get ready for the orders to flood in.'

Some of his joy dimmed. 'Yeah—going to be an interesting few months ahead.'

She couldn't fathom his shift in mood—not when he'd just launched both their companies into a new market. Unless he was concerned about his parents' reaction... But he'd said they were fine with him branching out.

Whatever the reason, she wished he trusted her as much as she trusted him.

'Are you going to expand on the collection?'

'Probably,' he said, his reticence complete as he took out his smartphone and scrolled down his to-do list. 'But for now we've got a final run through for the Hollywood glamour campaign scheduled.'

She could accept his reluctance to talk, could pretend it was okay he'd given her the brush-off without consequences. But they'd come too far to fake that all they shared was a meaningless fling. She might have no idea how to label what they had, but him demeaning it with his lack of trust was unacceptable.

'You've just nailed a preview show that could take your contemporary designs worldwide. So what's the problem?'

'No problem. I just can't afford to rest on this success when we have a major show coming up.'

Perfectly logical explanation. But his evasiveness was palpable. And it disappointed her more than she'd expected. Which could only mean one thing. She was in way over her head.

She didn't want to push him, didn't want to make a big deal out of this, but she'd vowed to live every moment to the max—and that meant confronting issues head-on, not skirting around them in the hope they'd vanish.

'Why won't you let me in?'

His thumb stilled over the smartphone and he finally raised his gaze after an eternity.

'What do you mean?'

'You need me to spell it out?'

With a typically male sigh of exasperation he thrust his phone back into his pocket and folded his arms.

'I care about you, Sapphire, but I've got too much on my mind to get into this now.'

If his posture didn't scream *back off*, the deep frown slashing his brows did. She guessed he expected her to be happy he'd admitted he cared. How magnanimous.

Though she had to agree with him. This probably wasn't the best place to discuss anything beyond work. Not if she wanted honest answers.

There'd be time for confrontation later, but the longer this went on she knew one thing. Patrick had grown on her, and having him walk away without giving him some indication of how she felt would be a travesty.

Letting him leave without the truth would be something she'd regret, and she was done living with regrets.

'Fair enough.' She shrugged as if it didn't matter, when in fact it mattered a great deal. 'You did good, by the way,' she said, standing on tiptoes to kiss his cheek. 'You should be proud.'

His stricken expression bamboozled her before he forced a smile. 'Thanks, I'll see you at Fourde later?'

'Count on it,' she said, wondering what had undermined this confident man to the point where he found praise uncomfortable, and knowing she'd never find out if he didn't trust her enough.

Mesmerised, Sapphie watched the Fourde Fashion show from a front row seat.

She'd envisaged the possibilities when Patrick had first had the Old Hollywood Glamour idea for the show, but never in her wildest dreams had she anticipated something so…so…*stupendous*.

Vibrant satin evening gowns in magenta, sapphire, crimson and gold, bias cut and strapless, highlighted by Ruby's exquisite creations and elbow-length ebony satin gloves.

Dramatic red lipstick, finger-waved hair and kitten heels.

Crisp white shirts tucked into high-waisted pants, hair parted on the side, lashings of mascara.

Models channelling Katharine Hepburn and Marlene Deitrich, classic elegance, bold statements.

Sapphie didn't know where to look first.

If she'd thought his contemporary show had been amazing, this one would shoot his reputation into the stratosphere.

And hers. Having the runway hit of Fashion Week would solidify Seaborns' success for years to come.

And she owed it all to Patrick.

He'd given her this opportunity, had believed in Seaborns despite the rumours and she couldn't thank him enough.

Maybe she could show her gratitude later, when they finally caught up outside of work for the first time in seven days. The snatched smooches and illicit touches beneath the boardroom table didn't cut it and she'd been clamouring for him all week.

How she'd survive—*physically*, she had to focus on physically—when he returned to Paris was beyond her.

No way would a gym workout hold half the appeal of a night in Patrick's arms.

Those arms… Never had she felt so secure than the times he'd wrapped her close, content to hold her. For an independent gal with no plans for marriage, let alone a relationship beyond dinner and fun nights, their closeness seriously shook her.

They'd developed a bond no matter how much they wanted to deny it.

So what now?

Back to business as usual for her—running Seaborns and trying not to run herself into the ground again. And back to Paris for Patrick.

What she wouldn't give to swap places with him…

In that moment the catwalk, the applause, the audience faded as an idea so shocking, so far out of left field, blew away every logical reason insisting they could never be together.

Go to Paris.

She shook her head, trying to dislodge the ludicrous idea. It didn't work. Instead the idea morphed, expanded, and presented a host of unwelcome possibilities she shouldn't acknowledge but couldn't ignore no matter how much she wanted to.

Logically, it wasn't possible. Even if she were to visit for a while, see how a potential relationship developed, would it ultimately change anything?

Old workaholic Sapphie insisted *not a chance*.

New revived Sapphie said '*you won't know unless you give it a go.*'

Confused, and a little shaken by an irrational surge of hope, she tried to mentally recite every reason why she couldn't do this.

Who would run Seaborns?

Well, Rubes had done a good job of it during those three months she'd had off.

Would there be a future in it?

She'd never know if she didn't try.

How would Patrick feel?

She'd have to ask him to find out.

And that was what had her angsty. She'd have to confront the guy she loved and see how he felt about her spending some time with him in Paris.

The guy she loved...

Uh-oh.

Somewhere between him barging into Seaborns, catching her in grungy workout clothes, and romancing her in style at the Langham she'd stupidly fallen in love with the guy.

A guy based in Europe.

A guy who'd gone out of his way to spell out the unlikelihood of a future.

Sheesh, he hadn't wanted to continue their fling for the two weeks after the hotel. What chance did she have of convincing him to give anything longer a go?

Logistically it would be a nightmare doing the long distance thing. And realistically how long could something like that last? A few months tops, before they moved on, caught up in their careers.

It might be nice to dream about, but on a practical level it couldn't happen.

Could it?

Sapphie glanced at the stage and caught sight of Patrick applauding the excited models as they passed him, the laugh lines around his eyes as familiar as the permanent wicked tilt to his lips.

Her motto after she'd left Tenang was to live in the moment more, to take calculated risks rather than playing the safe option all the time.

But there were risks and there were *risks*, and following Patrick to Paris on a whim in the hope he'd love her back...

That wasn't risky. That was downright certifiable.

CHAPTER NINE

PATRICK WOULDN'T ADMIT it to anyone but the backstage buzz at a fashion show really got him going. He couldn't thank his folks for much, but for unwittingly instilling a love of fashion into him? Yeah, he could be magnanimously grateful for that.

As Fourde Fashion's showstopper, a daffodil-yellow shimmering silk sheath that cascaded in layers from the waist to the floor, took to the stage a roar from the crowd filled the room.

Thunderous applause, standing ovation, photographers' flashes for the second time this week as Fourde Fashion wrapped up Fashion Week with a requested encore show reinforced what he'd known: this collection would be going places.

And so would he.

He'd done it. Put his past behind him once and for all. Vindicated the trust his folks had placed in him this time around. Proved he could take an untried entity and turn it into a winner. Which meant it was time. Time to confront his parents with his plans. Big plans.

Never in the history of Fashion Week had a house been asked to repeat their show, but that was exactly what had happened when the audience and media had gone wild for his Old Hollywood Glamour campaign earlier in the week.

His phone hadn't stopped ringing with congratulations and orders—so many orders for the gowns *his* idea had inspired.

This was the beginning. Next stop Paris, and he wouldn't stop until he'd gone all the way to the top.

Pity the only congrats he'd received from his folks consisted of a brief e-mail citing revenue projections if initial orders continued and a terse 'good show'.

It should have stung but it didn't. He'd done this for himself, to prove he had what it took to launch solo.

As much as he hated to admit it, albeit to himself, the failure of his first show all those years ago had left a lasting legacy.

Logic explained away that initial disaster as being a combination of factors—wrong show at the wrong time, too innovative, breaking out of an established mould, not delivering on a tried and true brand—but he'd be lying if he didn't admit to a sliver of doubt undermining his big plans for the future.

He wondered if his folks even remembered him mentioning his plans to leave the company and set up on his own. Doubtful, as unless anything he had to say involved Fourde Fashion they weren't interested.

No matter. They'd hear it soon enough when he confronted them shortly, for he had every intention of capitalising on the buzz surrounding his indie show to open his own label.

'We did it.' Sapphire sidled up to him, touched his arm, and he immediately wanted to bundle her into his.

'Never any doubt.'

Her eyes shone with pride.

'I wondered if we could pull this off.' When he raised an eyebrow she hurried on. 'I mean, your idea was amazing, but to squeeze in the contemporary show, then co-ordinate the clothes and the accessories for Fourde in a month, and make it look like that—' she gestured towards the models tittering in a huddle backstage '—nothing short of a miracle.'

'We're a good team,' he said, meaning it. She'd inspired him, both in and out of work, and for the hundredth time this week he wondered how he could walk away from her.

'This could be the first of many successful Fourde/Sea-borns collaborations?'

'About that...' He intertwined his fingers with hers and tugged her towards a quiet corner, away from sound and lighting technicians, models, dressers and neurotic designers.

There'd be no easy time to tell her and he'd rather she heard it from him.

'I'm leaving for Paris in two days.'

Shock widened her eyes. 'So soon?'

'Yeah—have to capitalise on this success while the entire fashion world is still talking about it.'

'Makes sense.'

He'd been worried how she'd take the news. Sure, they'd agreed on a no-strings-attached fling, but they'd grown closer than he'd expected. And the way she'd bailed him up after the indie show, asking why he wouldn't let her in...

Yeah, there were emotions at play here and this could get messy.

'My time in Melbourne has been great—'

'Maybe I could visit you in Paris?'

His heart leapt in exaltation, before logic slapped it down. Her making a trip to Paris to continue their fling wouldn't ultimately change anything. Their relationship had an end date and prolonging it would only make it more difficult.

He needed to focus on work for what was to come. The confrontation with his folks and the resultant fallout wouldn't be pretty. The paparazzi would have a field-day, plastering his proposed defection to start up his own fashion house to rival Fourde all over the media.

Then there were the actual set-up logistics: finding offices, showroom space, hiring staff, marketing plans... Yeah, he needed to be one hundred percent focussed, and having Sapphire alongside him in Paris would guarantee a major distraction he didn't need.

'For a holiday?'

He hated seeing her tentative joy at joining him in Paris crumple in the face of his deliberately cool response.

'For a few weeks. To see if…if we—'

'We've had a great time, but I'm going to be pretty busy in Paris for the next few months, so maybe you should postpone your holiday?'

The words tumbled out of him in a rush, harsh and confronting. He willed her to understand, to be grateful for the time they'd had together.

Pain lanced his chest as she yanked her hand out of his and stepped back, her accusatory glare filled with retribution.

'You don't want me to come,' she said.

The eerie monotone was as scary as her expressionless pallor. But he saw the shattered pain in her eyes, mirroring his.

'It's not that—'

'Then what is it?' Her metamorphosis from cool to furious happened in an instant. 'This thing between us moved beyond a fling ages ago, so for you to stand there and pretend what happened between us was just a convenient side benefit while we worked together—' She shook her head, her hair tangling like spun gold around her face. 'I'm such a moron.'

'Listen to me—'

'No!'

She lowered her voice when several people glanced their way. 'I'll drop by your office later to tie up loose ends but I don't want to hear another word about you and me. Got it?'

Damn it, he'd made a frigging mess of this. He needed to give her some snippet of truth because he couldn't leave her hurting—not like this.

'You're wrong. You mean everything to me—'

She bolted, her red-soled stilettos clacking against the floorboards, echoing the furious beating of his heart.

He could have sworn it pounded out a repetitive rhythm: *idiot…schmuck…jerk…*

* * *

Sapphie's first instinct to flee might have been a foolish one business-wise as she brushed off countless congratulations, but she had to get out of here. Had to find somewhere she could breathe without feeling as if she'd faint.

He didn't want her.

Tears burned the backs of her eyes as she exited the Melbourne Exhibition Centre, slipped off her heels, and joined the crowds strolling along the Yarra River's Southbank.

Anonymity was good. No one would give her a second glance on a busy Saturday night, when black-clad women dangling shoes off their fingertips wasn't all that unusual. Though they might stare if she bawled, so she swallowed her tears and walked. And walked.

Past the Crown Towers and casino, past the upscale Southbank restaurants, past the Langham Hotel. She practically ran past that landmark, her throat clogged with grief. For she *was* grieving. Grieving over the loss of Patrick, the guy she'd trusted enough to love, the guy who'd flung the lot back in her face.

Okay, she hadn't exactly told him she loved him but didn't the guy have half a brain? He knew how much Seaborns meant to her. She'd told him she'd almost ended up a basket case because of it. So the fact she'd wanted to follow him to Paris should have clued him in to how she felt.

Idiot. Him. Not her.

Actually, her too. For thinking for one second a guy like Patrick could change.

Just because he'd become a whiz-bang businessman didn't mean all those internet reports were behind him. For all she knew he'd schmoozed her as part of his business plan, adding her to the long list of women he'd bedded.

Harsh? Maybe. But it was a pretty good explanation for the way he'd thrown her away now their business association had come to an end.

However, as she reached St Kilda Road and turned left, crossing the bridge and ending up outside Flinders Street Station, she managed to calm down enough to view this rationally.

Patrick had never made any promises. In fact he'd gone out of his way to explain the short-term nature of their assignation. She'd known it, had acknowledged it, yet had gone ahead and fallen in love regardless.

Her bad, not his.

He'd done nothing wrong. They'd worked incredible magic together professionally and managed to combust a little personally.

She felt whole again, physically capable of taking on anything, and she had him to thank. Rather than berate him she should be thanking him.

All very logical, but it did nothing for the ache in her heart. Acknowledging the truth and accepting it were miles apart.

As she waited in a taxi rank, watching partygoers bustling around Federation Square opposite, she knew what she had to do.

Head home, meditate, get a little space and perspective, then drop by his office as planned and show Patrick Fourde how accomplished she was at moving on.

Easy.

If she could just get past the fact that after tonight she probably wouldn't see him again.

Patrick paced his office, blind to the lights of Melbourne spread out like diamonds on a cape many storeys below.

He should be on top of the world right now. Out with the team, celebrating their success. Solidifying his plans to expand. Maybe even rehearsing the spiel he'd need to give his folks to avoid them having coronaries.

Yet all he could think about was Sapphire.

The devastation in her eyes when he'd told her not to follow him to Paris. The pain twisting the lips he craved. Her disbelieving pallor.

They'd moved past a fling after that Langham weekend, yet he'd relegated what they'd shared to just that by dismissing her offer.

He knew how much it must have cost her to tell him, knew how much she prized Seaborns. For her to contemplate coming to Paris with him...

He cursed out loud.

It looked as if her feelings mirrored his.

Which meant...

He slammed a fist against the sideboard, watching Serge's globe and the stupid pins he'd stabbed into various countries jump.

How far he'd come from those days when he'd travelled the world schmoozing and partying, playing up to the reputation he'd deliberately courted after his first failure.

The opinion of so many had burned in his gut, never doused no matter how much alcohol he poured down his throat, never easing no matter how many beds he lay in

But judging from the reception his indie collection had received at Melbourne Fashion Week it was time to have another go at entering a market he knew he had a lot to offer to.

Interestingly, his folks had ignored the e-mail he'd sent them with links to press accolades for the indie collection.

Not that they could ignore it for too much longer, considering he had their meeting all planned out. Present the latest sales figures and projections, introduce his plans for a breakaway company, thank them and hand in his resignation.

It wouldn't be easy—far from it. Fourde Fashion was one of the oldest establishments in Europe. For the youngest son to go head to head with his parents...yeah, it would be tough. He could handle it—had handled being a focus of the media for years.

This time, though, he intended on being front and centre in the media for all the right reasons.

'Security let me up.'

Patrick turned, unprepared for the slash of sadness to his gut, which intensified as he caught sight of Sapphire striding across his office, head held high.

She'd changed into a pale blue leisure suit and let her hair down, managing to look coolly elegant and comfortable at the same time. Soft and approachable, at odds with the mutinous twist to her lips.

He'd expected her to be tentative and shaken when she showed up—not defiant with a battle gleam in her eyes.

'Let's get to work,' she said, flopping into the chair opposite his desk and flicking on her iPad. 'I assume I'll be liaising with Serge from now on?'

'Yeah,' he said, sitting opposite her, his hands curling into fists at the thought of Sapphire liaising with anyone but him. 'He's in charge in the interim.'

'Interim?' She typed, pretending his answer didn't mean anything, but he saw her shoulders tense.

''Til we figure out who's heading up the Melbourne branch permanently.'

It wasn't going to be him, once he'd vocalised his plans to his folks.

'That's it? You breeze in for a month, hit a major home run, and leave?' She continued typing, not looking up. 'Seems like a funny way to run a business. Especially when Fourde is trying to get a foothold in the Aussie market.'

'I know what I'm doing,' he said, wishing he could tell her all of it.

But he couldn't afford a leak. Not with so much at stake. This time he would do it right.

'Do you?' She finally glanced up, fixing him with a piercing glare that eviscerated. 'Because from where I'm sitting, it looks like you haven't changed a bit. Still flitting from one thing to another, searching for the next shiniest toy to play with, unable to settle.'

She'd nailed his past persona to a tee. *Past*. And the fact she thought him so shallow irked.

'There's a lot you don't know.'

'Enlighten me.'

She carefully placed her iPad on the desk and leaned forward, tapping the bulging manila folder containing their brainstorming. 'We did good with this. Real good. We're in every major fashion magazine around the world this week, not to mention the online forums and websites.'

She leaned back, folded her arms, so sure appealing to his business side would get him to change his mind.

'This could be the start of something great, so why are you running away?'

'You're not just talking about work here,' he said, knowing they needed to have this conversation but not prepared for it.

What could he say? That he had to launch his own company in Paris as vindication for the failures of the past? That he wanted his folks to sit up and finally take notice of him for once? That everything he'd done the past few years, working his butt off for Fourde, had been leading towards this moment?

He couldn't give it up—even for the only woman who had ever made him feel.

'You've made yourself perfectly clear but I don't get it.'

She spoke so softly he had to strain to hear the rest.

'We've connected on an emotional level and you have no intention of seeing it through.' She tapped her chest. 'I'm the one willing to travel to Paris to be with you, to see if there's any chance at a future, but you're not interested. And I guess my ego is demanding to know why not.'

He shook his head, frustrated with the situation, frustrated with *her*. If they'd connected, how come she thought so little of him?

The thought of them together in Paris appealed on so many levels. Except the one that mattered most—the one that said he couldn't afford to lose sight of the end goal, not now.

'Not everything's about you,' he said, hating the flash of pain in her bold gaze but needing to establish emotional distance before he caved. 'I'm heading back to Paris for business and you need to accept it.'

'We don't stay in touch? We pretend like we never happened?'

Her quiet stoicism slugged him hard. Classy to the end, she wouldn't rant or swear or blame. It would have been better if she had. He could have coped with histrionics. This quiet acceptance, as if she'd expected him to let her down all along, sucked big-time.

'I can't give you any promises. I have important stuff to do in Paris and that's my priority for now.'

'Stuff?' She made it sound as if he'd be dancing the can-can rather than launching a new business.

In that moment, despite his obsession with secrecy until his company went live, he knew he'd have to tell her to get her to back off. To understand. He wasn't toying with her. He just didn't want to make any promises he couldn't keep.

He'd been working too long and too hard to sacrifice his dream now.

'I'm launching my own fashion house.'

Her eyes widened in surprise and she stared at him as if he'd announced he'd be constructing the next Louvre by hand.

'It's confidential for now. You can probably appreciate the delicacy with being Fourde's rival.'

'Of course.' She nodded. 'Congratulations.'

Her voice sounded strangled and she couldn't meet his eye.

Great. He'd finally told her the truth and *this* was the reaction he got? Then again, he'd vetoed any possibility of a future between them so what did he expect? For her to throw a party?

'Well, then, I guess you go do your *stuff* and I'll do mine.'

She stood so quickly his head snapped back.

'Hand over to Serge tonight and I'll meet with him to-morrow.'

'But I thought—'

'What?'

She whirled on him with so much fury he wouldn't have been surprised if the air between them had crackled.

'You thought I'd sit here meek and mild tonight, being the good little business associate?'

She towered over him, hands on hips, brows drawn, eyes narrowed, magnificent.

'Newsflash. I've finally got your message loud and clear.'

For the second time that evening he found himself yelling, 'Wait…' to her retreating back as she ran from his office.

He swore, long and hard, a string of French and English curses that did little to ease the frustration pounding through his body.

Of course Serge chose that moment to saunter into his office, an aged double malt Scotch in one hand, ice bucket in the other.

'Looks like you could use one of these,' he said, laying both on the sideboard. 'Was that Sapphire I saw heading towards the elevators?'

'Shut the hell up,' Patrick said, stalking across the office to grab one of the glasses Serge had filled in record time.

'Hmm… I'm guessing you won't be liking this so much, then.' Serge grappled in his pocket for a moment, before pulling out a pin and sticking it in Melbourne on the globe. 'Look at this this way—she's another flag in your world domination.'

Patrick had never been a violent man, despite being pushed to the limits by his dad on numerous occasions, but at that moment, with Serge's smug grin taunting, he'd never felt like hitting anyone more.

'Leave. Now.'

Serge held up his hands. 'Thought you needed to lighten up. It's harmless fun—'

'Get out.'

Serge reached for the Scotch, took one look at his face and thought better of it, backing away instead.

'We can go over the latest orders in the morning.'

Patrick grunted in response, willing the fury making his hand shake to subside.

He wasn't angry with Serge so much as the situation. He hated feeling helpless, and watching Sapphire walk out had rendered him more powerless than he'd ever been.

He needed time and space to calm down. The bottle of Scotch wouldn't go astray either.

'Take it easy, *mon ami*,' Serge said, backing through the door with a final concerned frown.

Alone. Finally.

He downed the Scotch in three gulps and had poured another when the door flung open again.

'Dammit—'

'What did he mean, "she's another flag"'

Sapphire's voice was quiet, deadly, at odds with the shattered agony in her eyes.

The alcohol burned in his empty gut. His sudden nausea was more to do with explaining to Sapphire what that stupid globe meant than drinking on an empty stomach.

She jabbed a finger at him. 'I came back because I didn't want us to end like we did first time around, with me not saying what I should've.'

She toyed with the string on her hoodie and he hated that he was the cause of her stricken pallor.

'Back then I acted like an immature child. I should've taken your call and thanked you for seeing me home on graduation night, should've told you I appreciated you caring enough to bother after the way I treated you during our final year.' She shook her head. 'So that's why I'm here. I'd like to think I'm more mature these days and I should've congratulated you properly before. Shouldn't have let my feelings cloud your success. For that's what you'll be with your own company. I have no doubt.'

She shrugged. 'But after what I overheard maybe I should've left well enough alone, like in high school.'

He didn't speak and she hovered in the doorway, vulnerable in a way he'd never imagined.

'Tell me what Serge meant.'

He glanced at the inanimate object encapsulating the stupidity of his past and wondered why he'd kept it. He didn't need a reminder of how far he'd come. He stared at the reality in the mirror every morning while shaving. He wasn't the same person he'd once been. He'd become so much more through hard work and dedication.

'I'm not leaving 'til you tell me,' she said, her voice quivering. Something inside him broke.

In a pique of rage he swept the globe off the sideboard, sending it spinning onto the floor, surrounded by countless pins dotting the carpet.

She gaped, but didn't move, and he clenched and unclenched his fists several times before being able to speak.

'Sometimes any form of attention is better than none.' He kicked the globe. 'Serge and I were young. He came up with the stupid idea to…uh…catalogue our conquests according to location.'

Her sharp intake of breath killed him, but not half as much as the devastation crumpling her mouth.

'I never did, but Serge hung onto this, and after a while I used it as something to spur me on—a reminder of a past I didn't want to go back to. I channelled my energies into my work, hoping to gain recognition that way.'

'Did it work?'

'Still trying.'

As the words popped out he wondered if he'd ever feel truly vindicated. He'd taken Fashion Week by storm. Had provided a good launch-pad for his contemporary fashion house. Had garnered attention from around the world.

So why the emptiness deep down, in a place he'd expected to be filled once he'd done what he'd set out to do?

'You keep trying.' The shimmer of tears hit him hard. 'In the meantime, why don't you admit all I ever meant to you was another flag on your globe.'

He crossed the room in four strides and reached for her. 'You know that's bull. What we shared was really special.'

She shrugged out of his grasp. 'Yeah, so special you won't give us a chance.'

He wanted to explain but couldn't find the words. No other woman made him feel as perplexed, as out of his depth, as Sapphire Seaborn.

Confusion churned his gut as he struggled to articulate, and his true feelings hit at the same moment as she ran.

This time for good.

CHAPTER TEN

Sapphie didn't want to meet with Serge. She didn't want to set foot in the Fourde Fashion offices ever again. But her wishes didn't come into this.

She was doing it for Seaborns. She'd do anything for Seaborns. The one constant in her topsy-turvy life.

Managing the family business might have almost driven her into the ground, mentally, physically and emotionally, but it was still standing, resolute and dependable, while the rest of her life crumbled around her diamond-clad ears.

Continuing a business relationship with Fourde Fashion was a smart move. Thanks to the Fashion Week success Seaborns had enough orders to fill for the next decade. Only a fool would walk away from something so lucrative.

Besides, Ruby would be at this meeting too, and she had to act as if everything was fine. The last thing she needed was Rubes freaking out if she thought Sapphie was stressing over losing Patrick.

As she strode into the boardroom her business focus stalled. Memories did that to a girl. Memories she'd have to forget if she expected to get through this meeting without falling apart.

'*Bonjour*,' Serge said, bowing over her hand in the flamboyant way she'd come to expect whenever their paths crossed. 'How are you?'

'Fine.'

She made a mockery of the monosyllabic response by slamming her portfolio down a little too hard on the table.

Ignoring his questioning glance, she busied herself with setting up the data on her iPad and finding the figures they needed to go over for future projections.

His silence unnerved her but she kept busy. As long as she stayed busy everything would be okay. She could ignore the permanent ache in her chest and the sick emptiness in her belly.

According to Serge, Patrick had left. A day early. Caught a flight late last night. Could he have got away any faster?

She'd been up all night, wishing she hadn't run out on him. He'd been sincere about that stupid globe, had said she'd meant more to him than any other woman and she believed him.

So why was he hell bent on pushing her away?

She'd hoped to confront him today, without the heat of last night's emotions clouding the issue. Instead he'd brought forward his departure, pretty much telling her he'd meant it when he'd said they were over.

'Your sister is joining us?'

Sapphie nodded. 'Far as I know.'

'She's very talented.' Serge tapped the latest industry magazine cover, featuring Patrick's showstopper and Ruby's choker.

'Someone mention my name?' Ruby breezed into the room, the only person Sapphie knew who could pull off a pink poncho, purple velvet mini, black and white striped leggings and maroon ankle boots. 'Because I've got talent in spades, you know.'

'Modesty too,' Sapphie muttered as Serge laughed.

'Can you ladies give me a few minutes while I grab some stuff for our meeting?'

'Sure.' Ruby waved him away, her astute gaze zeroing

in on her, making Sapphie wish she'd cancelled this meeting after all.

Ruby dumped her portfolio on the table and plopped onto the chair next to her, waiting until Serge had left before elbowing her.

'What's going on?'

Sapphie took a deep breath. Convincing Rubes she was fine would take a monumental effort.

'What do you mean?'

Ruby rolled her eyes. 'I spoke to Serge a few hours ago. He said Patrick left.'

'No great surprise there.'

Ruby frowned. 'But I thought...'

'What?'

'That you two were in it for the long haul.' Ruby slung an arm around her shoulders and hugged. 'You okay?'

'Fine.' Her clipped tone suggested otherwise and Ruby sighed.

'What happened?'

'Nothing. He's going solo in Paris, launching a new company.'

Ruby's eyebrows rose as she sat back. 'He's a talented guy. The European scene won't know what's hit it.'

'Absolutely.'

And he hadn't told her about it—any of it—until she'd practically dragged it out of him.

Ultimately that was what had made her walk away last night. His lack of trust in her, his inability to confide in her after all they'd shared.

It had hurt more than she could have imagined.

Apparently short-term flings weren't privy to long term plans.

Ironic. She'd been hell-bent on confronting him this morning and demanding answers—she could thank her mum for her dogged determination too—but it had been too late.

She'd taken it as a sign. They were over. For good.

'You two were great together,' Ruby said, patting her hand. 'Professionally and personally.'

Sapphie *sooo* didn't want to have this conversation.

'Can we focus on work today—?'

'Serge said he's never seen Patrick like this—totally obsessed with a woman.'

Yeah, gaining that extra 'flag' would be enough to fuel any obsession.

'Rubes—'

'He hasn't dated for a year. Has focussed on making it big in this biz.' She frowned. 'Not that his parents care. He got shafted in Paris.'

Despite her wanting to put Patrick behind her, Ruby had piqued her curiosity.

'What happened?'

Ruby rubbed her forehead. 'Apparently his first show years ago was too cutting edge. Buyers rebelled. Cost Fourde megabucks. His parents distanced themselves and the company, treated him like a second-class citizen. So he's worked his ass off since—was the sole inspiration behind the Fourde spring collection, coming up with that unique twist on the Eighties. Fashion world went wild for it.'

'Like they did for Old Hollywood Glamour?'

'Exactly.' Ruby picked up a pen and doodled diamonds. 'Another employee took the credit. Patrick didn't tell his folks the truth.'

'No way?'

'Serge said they've got this screwy relationship.'

'I figured from what he told me.'

Ruby smirked. 'So you guys *did* manage to talk between other activities?'

Sapphie punched her in the arm.

'Explains why he's so determined on heading back to Paris.' Ruby tilted her head to one side, studying her. 'Don't you think this start-up company has a lot to do with proving his success to his folks?'

'Don't know. Don't care.'

'Liar,' Ruby said, swivelling to face her. 'Are you going after him?'

Sapphie stared at Ruby as if she'd suggested Sapphie steal the Crown jewels alone. 'Even if I were remotely interested any more, which I'm not, remember that business I run? Seaborns? Ring any bells?'

'I've run it before. I can do it again.' Ruby shrugged. 'You're obviously in love with the guy. Why don't you give a relationship a chance?'

'Because I don't—I can't—ah, hell...'

'Deep breaths, sis. It's not that hard, really.'

Sapphie sighed. 'I already told him I was willing to head to Paris for a while. See how things developed between us.'

Ruby squealed and clapped her hands.

'He said no.'

Ruby grabbed her hand. 'What the—?'

'Looks like launching his precious company is more important than what we shared.'

Ruby squeezed her hand, released it. 'You're both as bad as each other.'

Sapphie pointed at her ear. 'Did you hear a word I said? I was willing to follow him—'

'So why didn't you?'

'Because he doesn't bloody want me.'

Ruby shook her head. 'At some point in time both of you will need to stop hiding behind business and lay your hearts on the line.'

'That's not what I'm doing—'

'Isn't it?' Ruby gestured to the stack of work on the table in front of them. 'It's what you've always done, Saph. Put the business ahead of your own needs. Don't let it ruin what you could have with Patrick.'

When Sapphie opened her mouth to reiterate that Patrick didn't want her, Ruby held up her hand. 'And don't give me that bull about him not being interested. He's ga-ga over you.' She paused only long enough to draw breath before continuing, 'The guy's probably terrified. He's spent his life searching for approval he's never got from his folks. Maybe he's scared he won't measure up to your expectations? Maybe he's scared of failure? He failed workwise once. Maybe he doesn't want to stuff up with his new company? Or maybe he's scared of failing at a relationship with you—?'

'Stop.' Sapphie held up her hand. 'That's a heck of a lot of maybes.'

Ruby grinned. 'Here's another one. Maybe you should give over that six-month supply of Tim Tams you owe me.'

'What for?'

'That bet we made when he first arrived on the scene.' Ruby smirked. 'That you wouldn't last two weeks without getting up close and personal with the delicious Patrick.'

'You've got a memory like an elephant,' Sapphie muttered, relieved to be joking rather than contemplating her sister's outlandish encouragement to follow him to Paris.

Ruby rubbed her hands together. 'Now we've got my chocolate bikkie situation sorted, when are you leaving?'

So much for a reprieve.

'Rubes, drop it—'

'Jax is in South Africa for the next six weeks so I can hold the fort 'til then. You should go,' Ruby said, slipping Sapphire her mobile—to book a ticket, presumably. 'I've done this before, remember? It'll be a cinch.'

Handing over the reins of Seaborns to Ruby again wasn't the problem. Potentially having her heart broken by Patrick Fourde was one big problem waiting to happen.

But what if Ruby was right?

What if Patrick did love her?

What if he'd pushed her away deliberately for some warped rationale she had no hope of figuring out?

And, the doozy, what if she headed to Paris to lay her heart on the line once and for all?

As Patrick waited for his folks to wrap up a conference call with a buyer in New York he lounged in a Louis XIV chair next to his favourite window.

How many times had he sat here, waiting for his folks to give him a few seconds of their precious time? Hardy and Joyce, the toast of Paris and beyond, willing to do anything in the name of Fourde Fashion.

He'd always wondered how far they'd go for their company...and he'd found out the hard way. Interestingly, after his first disastrous show and the fallout, they hadn't spoken of it. Had swept it under their priceless antique rug as if it had never happened.

They'd never trusted him to run a show again until Melbourne, and that was probably only because of the distance from Paris and their low expectations. If he stuffed up in Australia who would care?

He'd shown them. Not only had he hit a home run, he'd landed on the front page of every fashion mag in Europe and beyond.

Old Hollywood glamour was the new catch cry and he knew knock-off designs would be in shows and shops worldwide in the upcoming season.

It pleased him, leaving the company on a high, having given something back to his parents, ensuring he'd made his mark at Fourde—a positive mark this time.

As he stared out over Paris and the exquisite view of the Montmartre district he couldn't wait to get this meeting underway.

It would be predictable. He'd tell them his plans, they'd

nod absentmindedly, ask a few questions out of politeness and leave him to it. Classic Fourde parenting.

It wouldn't matter if he strutted into their office wearing a satin sheath and stilettos. They wouldn't notice.

Who knew? Maybe his new company, in opposition to theirs—and grabbing consumer dollars—would finally make them sit up and take notice of their youngest son?

He'd make his fashion house succeed if it killed him. And that included accessorising with the right jewellery. Jewellery he'd scoured Paris for but had come up with nothing that matched the stunning creations by Seaborns.

If he wanted to succeed he needed the best, which meant he needed to talk to Sapphire. But he hadn't figured out how to do it in business terms without letting emotions cloud the issue.

'Patrick? You wanted something?'

Joyce's cultured accent sounded the same as ever: cool, clipped, closed. He'd never heard his mother sound warm or happy and it saddened him. Amazingly glamorous at sixty, one of the most envied women in the fashion world, but with an aloofness that underscored her timeless beauty.

He stood and headed towards the door that had opened on silent hinges. 'Hey, Mum.'

He kissed her cheek, not surprised when she bustled him through the door as if she had more important matters to attend to.

'Dad.' He nodded a greeting at his father, who glanced up from the spreadsheets scattered across his desk long enough for a reciprocal nod.

Joyce sat on a chaise and gestured him to a seat opposite. 'Do you have more projection figures from Fashion Week?'

Not *How are you? How was your flight? Congratulations on doing an amazing job in Melbourne*. Nope, straight to the point: how their number one baby, Fourde Fashion, was doing.

'I haven't come here to discuss that,' he said, picking imaginary lint off his trousers before realising how nervous he looked. 'I've got something to tell you.'

He'd finally captured his father's attention. Hardy pushed back from the desk, rounded it in three strides and took a seat next to Joyce.

'What's going on? Did that order from the mega department store fall through? Thought it was too good to be true—'

'I'm leaving Fourde's to start up my own fashion house.'

The rhythmic tick-tock of a grandfather clock filled the silence as his stony-faced folks stared at him as if he'd proposed they scale the Eiffel Tower in couture.

'I've already mentioned this before, and the time is right now.' He tapped his smartphone and pulled up the spread on his indie show. 'I had a test run at Fashion Week in Melbourne. The contemporary, edgy stuff I want to focus on. It was a hit.'

'Interesting concept.' His father studied the phone screen through narrowed eyes. 'Is it sustainable?'

Surprised by his father's apparent interest, Patrick nodded. 'From the positive feedback so far, I think so.'

Hardy swiped his finger across the screen, a frown denting his brow. 'These are good, but it takes more than modern concepts to build a company.'

Patrick had expected censure, not praise—however begrudging—and he eased into a smile. 'I'd like to think I've learned from the best.'

Hardy's bushy eyebrows bristled before he cleared his throat. 'Fourde has dedicated workers, that's for sure. If you put in the hard yards, who knows what can happen?'

Patrick knew. He'd be sitting across from his folks at the next premier fashion show, sharing top billing.

'Thanks, Dad. I'm grateful for the experience but I'm looking forward to the challenge.'

Concern bracketed Joyce's pursed lips as she glanced at

the phone screen. 'These designs are stunning, Patrick, but have you forgotten the disaster of your first show?'

'No, Mum, I haven't.' He refrained from adding, *It's what drove me every day.* 'Paris wasn't ready for funky and contemporary back then. It is now.'

His father nodded, thoughtful. And with this meeting working out better than he'd expected, Patrick ventured into uncharted territory. Having a real family conversation.

'Why did you leave me to take the fallout back then?'

There—he'd asked the million-dollar question. He'd bet their answer would be priceless too.

Joyce had the grace to blush as she fiddled with a ruffled lace cuff and Hardy looked plain embarrassed. 'You were new to the business. Any adverse publicity wouldn't affect you as much as it would the company. We chose to protect the company.'

How noble. At the expense of their son.

His mum piped up. 'And we were right. Everything blew over. You returned to work, the company absorbed the financial losses and we moved on.'

They made it sound so simple, compartmentalising everything into a neat box. The disaster might have *blown over* for them, but he'd spent years trying to outrun the laughing stock he'd been made out to be in the press—had portrayed himself as a slick playboy to prove he wasn't the worst in the business. Gaining attention from all the wrong sources when he should have captured the attention of the two people standing before him now.

'I guess we've all moved on,' he said, sliding his phone back into his pocket. 'I'd like to resign—effective immediately.'

Joyce's perfectly plucked brows arched. 'That soon?'

He nodded. 'I want to capitalise on the buzz surrounding my Melbourne indie show.'

A loaded glance he had no hope of interpreting passed

between his parents before his father sagged onto the nearest surface—his desk.

'Before you go, there's something we need to discuss.'

Here it came. A counter-offer? A buy-out before he'd begun?

'We recently learned *you* came up with the spring collection concept.' Hardy shook his head. 'Why didn't you say something?'

How could he explain that pride had kept him silent? That he'd hoped his parents would recognise his signature talent? That even though his first collection had tanked for being innovative before its time, some of the same flair had been evident in those spring gowns? That even when he did voice his ideas they rarely deemed him worth listening to?

He could have said so much, but after a lifetime of their not being interested in what he had to say what would be the point now?

'Because ultimately it wouldn't have changed anything.' He thrust his hands in his pockets and took a few steps, pacing, before he stopped. He had nothing to be uncertain about. 'My plan was always to leave. I wanted to do the best job I could before that happened.'

'Then why did you take on the CEO role in Melbourne?' His mother laid a cerise-taloned hand on his forearm.

'Same reason.'

Not entirely true, but his folks didn't need to know his number one reason for nailing that show in Melbourne: proving to himself he could do it.

'The Hollywood glamour campaign was a perfect fit for Fourde Fashion, and if I hadn't worked here all these years, surrounded by the elegance this label stands for, I never would've been inspired to come up with something like that. So thank you.'

Joyce patted his forearm and Hardy straightened in what Patrick could only label as pride.

'You've given me an amazing start in this business, and I'll always be grateful, but my vision for the future isn't a good match for the Fourde brand—as we discovered the hard way. So it's time we part ways.' As he said the words he realised that they were true. They *had* given him an amazing start to the business. And perhaps even a start in changing the future of his relationship with them.

'There's nothing we can say to change your mind?'

Patrick shook his head. 'That's flattering, but no.'

That was when he saw the first real sign of emotion from his mother ever. Tears glistening and pooling in her artfully made-up eyes. Her vulnerability was shocking and frightening at the same time.

'I wish you luck, son,' she said, her voice quivering but her posture ramrod-straight.

Hardy held out his hand. 'Me too, son. You've done us proud.'

Ironic that it took him leaving the company for his father to articulate what he'd wanted to hear all along. What he'd wanted since he was a kid. A little attention.

'Just so you know, I'm going to put a positive spin on this in the media. Talk up Fourde, make this a personal decision so we don't face too much fallout.'

'Thanks.' Joyce's slight nod reminded him of a queen acknowledging a recalcitrant subordinate.

He'd done it.

He was on his own.

Time to instigate proceedings—starting with securing the best in the jewellery business.

He needed to talk to Sapphire.

His parents might have given their approval and finally acknowledged he had talent, but Sapphire had supported him all along. Had taken a risk on him. Even after he'd made her life impossible in high school and they hadn't spoken in ten years she'd taken a chance on his indie collection when she didn't have to.

And she'd still been willing to support him—to the extent she would have followed him to Paris.

What had he done? Deliberately pushed her away.

He'd been so wrapped up in proving he could do this on his own he'd lost sight of the bigger picture. A picture that had an amazing woman who complemented him right by his side.

Not wanting to be distracted from achieving success and the ultimate vindication in going it alone was one thing.

But not taking a chance on letting Sapphire get close because he half expected her to let him down eventually too was foolish.

She'd stood by him after he'd barged into her life just over a month ago when she really hadn't had any reason to.

He could rationalise away her loyalty as being for the Fourde Fashion name, but that didn't explain her devotion to making his contemporary collection succeed.

That had been about him, all about him, and she'd backed him regardless.

The kind of devotion she'd displayed was beyond rare.

Confronting his folks, vocalising his plans, had ensured one thing.

He was about to make his dreams come true.

The question was could he convince Sapphire to join him for the ride?

Sapphie rushed into the elaborate foyer of Fourde Fashion, slowing when her heels struck marble. Ruby had told her to break a leg during her Paris trip. Her sister hadn't meant literally.

She'd completed her third lap of the foyer when Patrick emerged from the wrought-iron elevator, striding for the glass front doors as if he had a million demons on his tail.

He had the long strides of a guy with places to be, but gone was the half-smirk, half-grin—the kind of daredevil smile women found infinitely appealing and that he'd used to great effect over the last month.

The way he looked now... Pensive. Driven. Tense. It sent her already thriving nerves into overdrive.

'Patrick?'

He stopped and swivelled as she stepped out from behind a marble column, his expression incredulous.

'What are you doing here?'

'We needed to talk so here I am.'

He stared at her as if he couldn't quite believe she was real and his mouth relaxed into that sexy smile. 'Guess I should've expected it.'

Sapphie didn't know if that was a good or bad thing. The fact he seemed pleased to see her was a plus. The fact he hadn't touched her yet? Big fat minus.

'Can we go somewhere private?'

He winked. 'So that's why you really came to Paris?'

She rolled her eyes. 'You're such a guy.'

'Sue me.' He gestured for her to step out through the door first. 'Come on, there's a little café around the corner.'

So far so good. At least he hadn't run screaming. Now to make him listen and hope to hell he'd tell her the truth.

They didn't speak, but she caught him sneaking glances at her and she self-consciously tugged at her leopard-print trench, winding her black cashmere scarf tighter.

She'd headed for Fourde straight from the airport, desperate to see him before she lost her nerve, so she hadn't seen much of Paris beyond the frame of a taxi window.

Now, as he ushered her towards an outdoor table at a cosy café tucked between an art supplies store and a shoe shop, she registered the fact she was in *Paris*. With a gorgeous guy.

It had been a secret fantasy when Patrick had first absconded all those years ago: imagining herself here, having fun, no responsibilities.

She'd resented him as time passed, envisaging him whooping it up while she threw herself into university studies and assisting her mum in her limited 'free' time.

After a while she'd deliberately forgotten him, wiping him from her mind, but every time she'd heard a mention of France, or had an illicit chocolate croissant treat or celebrated another Seaborns success with the finest French champagne, she'd remember him.

And wonder what might have been if he hadn't run.

'I want to know the real reason you didn't want me to come here.'

She fired the question before he'd sat down and he stared at her in disbelief.

'Can't a guy order an espresso before the inquisition starts?'

'Make it a cappuccino, throw in a *macaron*, and I'll give you a few seconds to compose some believable excuses.'

He chuckled, and it gave her hope that maybe this trip hadn't been a massive waste of time after all.

She waited until he'd placed their order and sat before leaning her forearms on the table and eyeballing him.

'Care to enlighten me?'

'Actually, I was planning on contacting you so we could talk—'

'Sure you were.' She took a deep breath and plunged on. 'Look, I didn't come all this way to stuff around. I want us to have an honest, adult conversation about why you pushed me away. And I'm not leaving Paris 'til you tell me the truth.'

His eyes narrowed. 'I don't do ultimatums all that well.'

'Yet you were quite happy to do me.'

Shock tightened his mouth. 'Crassness doesn't do you justice.'

'Oh, come on,' she said, throwing her hands in the air in exasperation. 'Can't you see I'm trying to snap you out of this stupor you seem to be in?' She slammed her palms on the table, not caring when several people glanced their way.

'How did your folks take the news of your impending departure from the family bosom?'

The tension pinching his lips eased. 'Surprisingly well.'

'That's great.' Seeing his softening had her hand snaking across the table, her fingers touching his. 'In case you haven't figured it out, dummy, I wouldn't have flown all this way unless I was in love with you, and I'll do whatever it takes to give us a fighting chance to see if we can make this work.'

Her chest heaved with the effort of blurting all that in one go and she inhaled deeply, willing him to say something— anything—rather than stare at her with a disheartening mix of wariness and shock.

'You love me?'

She would have laughed at his stunned expression if her heart hadn't been in her mouth. 'That's the general gist.'

'I was coming to see you... I didn't think... I mean, it's all so complicated...'

So complicated. But he'd been coming to see her. That had to be a good thing, right? Especially when he'd effectively ended it in Melbourne.

'What's complicated?'

He dragged a hand through his hair, tugged on his collar, loosened his tie—anything to out off answering.

'You being with me right now.'

'Isn't that my choice to make?'

A camera flash went off at a nearby table and he jumped. 'See that? Just the beginning. I've lived through media scrutiny before. It's tough—really tough. I wouldn't be willing to put you through the stress of it.'

Okay, so he was looking out for her. That meant he cared. Cared enough to give her up rather than put her through whatever he thought she couldn't handle. But she still didn't understand what it was.

'Thanks, but I'm a big girl. I can take care of myself.'

'Wasn't that the problem before, when you wound up at

that health spa? You tried to take care of everything and ended up getting ill?'

She frowned, more embarrassed by her foolishness in letting the situation get that out of hand than how fragile she'd been.

'That was physical exhaustion from pushing my body too hard. I learned from it. Changed. That's what people do—learn from their mistakes.'

Look at you, she wanted to say. This power-driven, determined entrepreneur was far removed from the laid-back goof-off he'd once been.

But now wasn't the time to bring up high school. She wanted answers to the here and now.

'I'm not the same person I was twelve months ago, and I'm guessing you're not either.'

He folded his arms and leaned back. 'Let me guess. Dear old Serge blabbed about the spring collection.'

'He might've mentioned it to Ruby, who told me.' She wrinkled her nose. 'I'm sorry that your parents had such a problem with you. They should have your name up in lights after scoring two major coups in a year.'

'It's no big deal.'

But it was. She could see it in the slight slump of his shoulders, the downturned corners of his mouth.

And it broke her heart to see an amazingly gifted guy like Patrick not being recognised for his talents.

'Then I think you've made a stellar decision in branching out on your own. The fashion world's going to love you.'

'Like you do?'

He spoke so softly she had to strain forward to listen.

'I never thought…' He shook his head and looked away.

'Thought what?'

He dragged his gaze back to hers, the hint of vulnerability buoying her hope. 'That someone like you could love someone like me.'

In that moment it all clicked into place—his reasons for pushing her away.

Thanks to his parents' chronic neglect over the years he didn't think he was good enough.

The thought that they'd bruised his self-esteem to such an extent made her want to march back to Fourde Fashion and tell them a few harsh home truths.

'Listen to me. You're the most amazing man I've ever known. You're smart and funny and gorgeous. And you have more creative flair in your little finger than half the people in this business. Surely you know that?'

He shrugged. 'The fallout from my first show was nasty. I got savaged in the press, shunned by aficionados for a while—'til I started playing their game. Attending their parties. Living their lifestyle. Going it alone I'll risk alienating a lot of people again. Sure you want to be part of that?'

Swallowing the rising lump in her throat because he cared that much, she flexed her biceps. 'Thanks to you, I'm stronger now than I've been in years. You've made me more energised and more alive than I could've hoped for. So whatever you face—count me in.'

'What about Seaborns? It's your life.'

'My life is wherever you are.'

'Careful, I see a violin quartet heading our way,' he said.

His dry humour was one of the many things she loved about him.

Sapphire Seaborn loved Patrick Fourde.

Who would've thought it?

'That's why you ran, isn't it? You expected the *merde* to hit the fan once you'd broken away from the family business and you didn't want me exposed to it?'

'Actually, it's also to do with the fact I needed to do this on my own.' He sighed. 'Last time my folks had to handle the fallout. This time I didn't want anyone else to take the flak but me.'

'Want to know something? Going it alone can be incredibly exhilarating. When you're successful, you're flying. It's an incredible rush. But then there are other times when it's nice to have people along for the ride.' She tapped her chest. 'How do I feel in here? Invincible, with you by my side.'

A hint of wariness still hovered. 'That's a hell of a responsibility for a guy to handle.'

She blew out an exasperated breath. 'I meant I'm stronger than I've ever been. How you make me feel empowers me.' Her hand gestured at the space on her right. 'I don't need you here all the time to feel good, but it's a lot more fun when you are.'

A glimmer of a smile eased the tension lines bracketing his mouth. 'You're a lot ballsier now than you were in high school. I like it.'

'Don't you mean love?'

He took an eternity to answer, literally leaving her on the edge of her seat.

'Walking away from you proved that,' he said, pinching the bridge of his nose before pinning her with a stare that snatched her breath. 'Only a dumb guy in love could rationalise himself into walking away from the best thing to ever happen to him.'

She sank back into her chair, sporting a goofy grin. 'You love me, huh?'

'Oh, yeah.' He grinned right back at her, but it faded too soon. 'This could get tough. Launching a new fashion house in Europe is highly competitive, and throw in the angle that I'm going up against family? Paparazzi will have a field-day.'

'So? All publicity is good publicity, right?' Sapphire waved away his concern. 'Know what I say? Bring it on—because Patrick Fourde is headed for the stars and nothing can stop him.'

He stared at her, wide-eyed. 'You have that much faith in me?'

She nodded and snagged his hand across the table. 'Absolutely. I made the mistake of not believing in you once. Never again.'

He squeezed her hand. 'You thought I was a no-good lout in high school.'

'No, I thought you were the hottest rebel I'd ever seen and I envied you beyond belief.'

'Why?'

'Because I wanted to be like you. Carefree. Cool. No responsibilities. I hated the fact you were so popular and didn't seem to work at it, while I was this rich nerd girl who had her whole life mapped out.' She giggled nervously. 'I developed a crush, and that only added to my angst. Because no way could I risk you finding out—'

'So you pushed me away instead?'

Sheepish, she shrugged. 'I had no choice in Biology, because we had to work together, but the rest of the time? Yeah, being around you was tough.'

The cocky grin spreading across his face was familiar and welcome. 'Must've been…pretending you didn't like me while wanting to jump me.'

'It wasn't like that.' She blushed. ''Til that kiss…'

'Lucky we made up for lost time in Melbourne recently,' he said, lifting her hand to his mouth to brush kisses across her knuckles, setting her latent desire for him alight.

'You know, I've heard Paris is the most romantic city in the world.' She glanced around, taking in the centuries-old buildings, the paved paths, the lovers strolling arm-in-arm. 'We should put it to the test.'

'You sure about this? Putting Seaborns on hold? Trialling a relationship among the frenetic pace of launching a new business?'

She should be glad he was putting her first. Instead all she could think about was holing away with him in some tiny, cosy garret with wine and pastries and boxes of condoms.

'Ruby is running Seaborns for the next six weeks 'til we figure out where this is going. And I'm hoping you'll want our jewellery for all your upcoming designs. As for the rest? I'm with you all the way.'

He let out a whoop that had passers-by glancing at them with indulgent smiles. Romance was commonplace in Paris after all.

'How about we take the coffee and *macarons* to go?'

'*Oui*,' she said, standing before he'd barely finished the question.

He pulled her into his arms, holding her as if he'd never let go.

Fine by her.

'You know my new venture will need the best accessorising money can buy?' he murmured in her ear, nibbling the lobe and shooting sparks through her body. 'How would you feel about taking Seaborns global? Or at least to France?'

'You're full of brilliant ideas,' she said, thrilled he'd arrived at the same solution she had on the long flight over here. 'And here's one for you.'

She stood on tiptoes and whispered in his ear what she'd do to him in the privacy of wherever they were staying.

They never did get to have their coffee and *macarons*.

EPILOGUE

PATRICK WASN'T A fan of long distance relationships. There was only so far Skype and a phone could go, despite his girlfriend being the most inventive woman he'd ever met.

He'd always known Sapphire had hidden depths, and he was eternally grateful he was the guy she'd chosen to plumb them.

Though there *was* an upside to long distance. The reunions. Over the last twelve months they'd snatched time together in Melbourne, Paris and once halfway in Singapore for a long weekend.

Their individual schedules had been manic but they'd survived. And tonight he'd repay her trust in him.

True to her word, she'd stood by him. Her faith in his capabilities was rock-solid.

His company had swept the buyers off their feet during the spring, summer and autumn collections. He'd graced the cover of every glossy magazine worldwide, and his company's designs had been seen on the red carpet from Cannes to Hollywood.

Accolades had ranged from *'Ahead of his time'* to *'Pure design genius'*. *'Bold.'* *'Innovative.'* *'Hip.'*

Supermodels clamoured to wear his clothes. Actresses proudly strutted to awards ceremonies in his contemporary designs.

The same magazines that had so harshly labelled him over a decade earlier now ran features on his clothes.

The entire world now knew who Patrick Fourde was—an entity in his own right.

He'd made it. Achieved his goal.

Now for the next challenge.

'Where are we?' Sapphire snuggled into his side, content to stare at him more than their surroundings.

'Home.'

One word that filled him with pride and warmth.

He'd never really had a home—not a place where he felt he belonged.

That would all change with this incredible woman, starting now.

A cute little frown creased her brow. 'This is your new place?'

'*Our* new place,' he said, keeping a firm hold on her with one arm while sliding a box out of his other pocket. 'This comes with it.'

Her mouth made a cute little O of surprise as she stared at the box.

'A wise woman once told me at my first solo fashion show in Paris that accessories make anything special,' he said, flipping open the box with great deliberation.

His choice in engagement ring, secretly designed by his future sister-in-law, was vindicated by Sapphire's sharp intake of breath.

'So a house like this needs a good proposal.'

And there, in front of an eighteenth-century apartment just off the Rue du Monde, he knelt in front of the woman he adored.

'Will you marry me, Sapphire Seaborn? Live in our home? Accessorise our marriage with a bunch of kids?'

'Kids aren't accessories,' she said in mock outrage while

her eyes glistened with tears. 'I can see I'll have to accept your proposal and set you straight.'

'Is that a—?'

'Of course it's a yes,' she said, dragging him to his feet and flinging herself into his arms. 'Yes, yes, *yes*!'

They kissed as if there was no tomorrow—wild and passionate and unhinged.

When they eventually disengaged he slid the diamond-encrusted sapphire onto her ring finger. 'You're the love of my life.'

'And I have the ring to prove it,' she said with a jubilant yell, holding her hand at arm's length to admire it. 'Best. Accessory. Ever.'

'Considering my future wife owns a jewellery store, there'll be plenty more where that came from,' he said, sliding his arms around her waist. 'Complimentary, of course.'

'Sure—as long as my future husband keeps me in a lifetime of exclusive couture,' she said, straight-faced.

'We make a great team, sweetheart.'

She kissed him in absolute agreement.

* * * * *

MODERN™

INTERNATIONAL AFFAIRS, SEDUCTION & PASSION GUARANTEED

My wish list for next month's titles…

In stores from 17th May 2013:

- ❏ The Sheikh's Prize— Lynne Graham
- ❏ His Final Bargain — Melanie Milburne
- ❏ Diamond in the Desert — Susan Stephens
- ❏ A Greek Escape — Elizabeth Power
- ❏ Princess in the Iron Mask — Victoria Parker

In stores from 7th June 2013:

- ❏ Forgiven but not Forgotten? — Abby Green
- ❏ A Throne for the Taking — Kate Walker
- ❏ A Father's Secret — Yvonne Lindsay
- ❏ Too Close for Comfort — Heidi Rice

Available at WHSmith, Tesco, Asda, Eason, Amazon and Apple

Just can't wait?

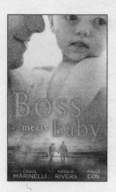
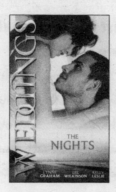